THUNDER SNOW

MIMI FOSTER

DEDICATION

This book is dedicated to my very own superhero, my husband, David Feith. There are no words to express how deeply appreciative I am of his unwavering love and support and encouragement. He loves me so much that he read this romance novel from cover to cover (committed love, indeed). His infinite patience and interaction in sharing ideas and scenarios has made this finished product possible.

This series contains adult content and is intended for mature readers.
Each of the five books in the Thunder on the Mountain series is a complete,
stand-alone story.

Thunder Snow (Contemporary – Book 1)
Thunder Struck (Contemporary – Book 2)
Thunder Storm (Contemporary – Book 3)
Jordan's Gift (Historical – Book 4)
Willow's Secret (Historical – Book 5)

In *Thunder Struck,* Jordan and Brandan discover century-old
journals. I was so enamored with the people who wrote the journals
(the original Jordan and her daughter Willow), I decided to write
their stories. Preferring conflict to come from external sources
rather than the relationship, this series is fun, tender, and
deliciously steamy.

PRAISE FOR MIMI FOSTER BOOKS

Absolutely my favorite

This is the best book I've ever read. I couldn't put it down! Loved the mystery surrounding Jack. He was a genuine romantic and from the beginning Callie fell in love with his rather rough exterior. They are the perfect couple.

Mary Rath on THUNDER SNOW

Absolutely and utterly Brilliant!! MUST READ!!!

I cannot even begin to tell you how much I LOVED this book!! Every single moment and every single page was like Christmas morning. Jordan and Brandan are two of the most beautifully developed and wonderfully written characters. Ms. Foster, you are now on my MUST READ ANYTHING YOU WRITE list!!

Amazeballs Book Addicts on THUNDER STRUCK

It just gets better and better

This series is positively addictive. It's kind of like giving heroine to an addict. Once you start the stories in this series you just can't put them down.

Joyce Ruskuski on THUNDER STORM

Truly a Gift

Mimi Foster continues to capture my imagination with warm and sensual characters, enchanting settings, and beautiful romance. Jordan and Edward are magnetic, and the non-stop fire between them kept me sizzling page after page!

P. Stachel on JORDAN'S GIFT

Best. Book. Ever.

A beautiful story that captured life and captured me. Foster captured how many of us are when we are alone, when no one is looking. When we don't like what or who we see when we look in the mirror but someone else can see our beauty. This is absolutely one of the best books ever.

Anne Marie Smith on <u>*MAISY'S MIRROR*</u>

CONTENTS

Chapter One
NEDERLAND

*E*arly autumn in the Colorado high country is as enchanting as anywhere on earth. Even in my exhaustion, the sun setting behind the Rockies as I wound my way through Boulder Canyon taunted me with the promise of escape. It was only an hour drive from the heart of Denver to the hamlet of Nederland, but the last few miles to my temporary refuge took a toll and, with it, the last of my hard-won stamina.

The key to my father's mountain retreat, affectionately known as his *Fortress of Solitude*, was waiting for me at the Amber Rose. I was captivated as I pulled in front of the rustic diner, and excitement warred with fatigue to help me summon the strength to get out of my car.

Bone weary, I pushed the door open to the jingle of bells. Two men, one on each side of the counter, turned to see who had disturbed their conversation. The leather-faced proprietor, who probably wasn't as old as he looked, assessed me with an effortless grin. That must be Sam.

The other man was tall, distinctly attractive, with wavy brown hair that brushed his collar. 'Electrifying' was the word that came to mind when I saw the blue of his eyes. I knew about sudden lightning strikes in the mountains, but did they also happen inside? Not wanting to stare, I commanded my body to move across the time-worn oak floor and felt a genuine welcome by the older, grizzled stranger.

"Hi, I'm Callie. I'll be staying at the Weston place for a while. I came for the key, and maybe a cuppa coffee?"

The wrinkled man with the sunken eyes and furrowed brow briefly reminded me of a bloodhound. He beamed as he took my hand in both of his calloused ones and worked it up and down.

"I thought you'd never make it. My name's Sam. Friends around these parts call me Wicked Sam, not 'cuz of my soul, but seeing as how I got such a wicked sense of humor." His endearing manner put me immediately at ease and made me confident that coming here was the right choice.

Turning toward the patron leaning casually against the bar, I wondered if that confidence was premature. With my brain wiped cleaner than a blackboard, I wasn't in any mood to figure out why it didn't feel as calm and relaxing as it had just a few moments before. The last thing I needed was to notice the cut of his jaw and how nicely he filled out his well-worn shirt. Nodding dismissively, I turned back to the friendlier character behind the counter.

"I've heard nice things about you, Sam. I'm anxious to spend time here finding out if they're true," I teased. Holding up my thermos, I asked, "Do you have enough to fill this? I'm running out of steam fast."

"Sure thing. I just made a fresh pot for Jack here." He snickered as he headed to the kitchen. "Be right back."

Mustering the smile I'd perfected over the years to appear genuine, I took a deep breath and braced myself to engage the delectable stranger, then mentally cringed for such a thought. My gaze locked on his cobalt eyes, and I was sure something had addled my usually competent brain. I was coming here to get away from men, and this one looked like he could be king of the unreasonable hill.

"Hi, I'm Callie," I said, hoping my hand didn't shake as I

extended it toward the handsome but formidable man. That was a stupid thing to do. I certainly didn't need to be touching him, but there was no need to worry. He merely looked at it indifferently.

"So I heard," was his sullen response.

"You live here in town?" I asked, trying to thaw his icy manner.

"Yep," was as much as I could extract from his perfect mouth. What a ridiculous thought. What the hell was the matter with me?

"Been here long?" I was usually adept at engaging strangers.

"Yep."

"Are you always this friendly?"

Not a move, not a twitch, just a brooding stare.

Sam came out with two mugs and a steaming pot of coffee.

"Changed my mind, Sam," Jack said. "Catch you tomorrow."

The bells sounded again as he opened the door. Before leaving, he impaled me with his razor-sharp glare. "You related to Charles?"

"So I heard." I grinned, knowing somehow he wouldn't be pleased with my repetition of his response. One last piercing glance from those azure eyes and he was gone.

"Whew," I said, smiling at Sam. "What kind of an immovable object was that?"

"Don't pay no attention to him, he don't mean no harm. Jack Franklin's about one of the nicest folks you'll ever wanna meet. He's good people, helps anybody who needs it. He don't normally go around yapping his trap much."

Taking a warm sip, I smiled. "I'll have to take your word on that."

Sam chuckled. "I heard from your pa. Got your key right here," he said, sliding it across the highly polished counter. "You turn left when you get to the back of my building, then take the road up about a mile. It'll be your only drive to the left. Can't miss it."

"Thank you. I'm drained right now. Hope you don't mind if I take off."

"No doubt, pun'kin. We're gonna be good friends, we got plenty of time." Filling my thermos with the last of the pot, he said, "That should help you 'til you get done what you need to get done tonight. Now get on down the road. Time for me to close up here."

I squeezed his hand, then made the drive up the back trail, thinking again of the events that finally led me to this shelter. This hidden sanctuary would be mine while I tried to figure out the mess that had become my life. Pulling into the drive, I was sure I'd taken a wrong turn. This was no cabin in the woods. When the key turned and the door opened, I was stunned. It was simultaneously a tranquil yet breathtaking work of art. It felt a lot like the first time I'd seen a house built by my favorite architect, Montgomery.

How had my father kept this little secret from me? That old coot. Who knew he had it in him? Everything about it called to the depths of my soul. I'd call first thing in the morning and tell him he was sitting on a gold mine - as if he didn't already know. There were touches here and there of my mother with a few of her favorite knick-knacks on display, but overall, it was pure passion.

Enthralled, I stood in the doorway trying to absorb the sensations. My job as a real estate agent had trained me to impersonally take in the essence of a building within the first minute of entering. But several minutes passed as I studied the play between rock, wood, polished and unpolished granite, and glass. No other architect I'd encountered had the ability to build into his surroundings like Montgomery, and I couldn't imagine this was the work of anyone else.

There was no part of me that remained detached. I couldn't find my impartial eye to study the structure because there was so much reverence involved. I wondered momentarily how my dad had snagged such a coup. Montgomery was several years out on his projects, and if this wasn't one of his, I was excited to find out who had designed it. Tomorrow would be soon enough to explore, but tonight I was thankful for this haven.

IT WAS THE BEST NIGHT'S SLEEP I'D HAD IN AS LONG AS I COULD

remember. The crisp mountain air and a feeling of safety for the first time in ages brought a much-needed rest. If it hadn't been for the alluring design of the shower pulling at me like a siren's call, I'm not sure I would've gotten out of bed.

The shower followed the line of the mountain it was built on. The glass enclosure extended in a delightful curve and gave it an atmosphere of being in the middle of nature, making it an oasis on its own. Water cascading from the shower head mimicked a waterfall and could be turned to feed into the deep blue tub below. It was a strange feeling to be able to look over the mountain range in the distance. Cleverly situated, there was no possible way anyone could see in.

Remnants of stress washed away as I lathered my fatigued body. Not for the first time I wondered why doing the right thing was so grueling? I'd lost so much - the home I loved, my best friend, my business had suffered, and for what? Pressing charges and going through a trial, and the perpetrator wouldn't even spend as much time in jail as it had taken to get him there.

The sound of the metallic click of the handcuffs grabbing his wrists yesterday morning echoed again through my mind. The deputy had him almost out of the courtroom when Jason suddenly turned. He hadn't said a word, but the threat was implied in his glare as he was pushed through the doorway.

Stepping out of the soul-refreshing steam, I shook off the dark memory and caught a glimpse of myself in the mirror. The marks on my body had disappeared, and I liked what I saw. It strengthened my resolve to never again be anyone's victim.

It was over. I was safe. The magical splendor of the surroundings called my name and made me feel like a woodland nymph. I'd long wanted to build my own place, but I'm not sure anything could match this exquisiteness. I dried my hair quickly and tied it back with a ribbon. Dressed in comfortable clothes, I packed my camera and headed to town with a lightness of spirit I hadn't known in years. I'd see if Sam had suggestions for a rookie hiker who was set on becoming an accomplished photographer.

The weather was perfect and life was full of new promise. Sitting at the counter, I had the first of what I figured would eventually be several hundred cups of coffee in this place. Sam set a fresh loaf of warm bread and cinnamon honey butter irresistibly in front me. It was cozy. I was glad I was here.

JACK WAS TROUBLED THAT MORNING WHEN SHE WALKED INTO THE Amber Rose like a regular. It was only the second time she'd been there, but he didn't want her getting too comfortable or feeling like she was going to be welcome.

He was conscious of the fit of her jeans as she raised her lithe body onto the stool at the counter. Ordering coffee, her soothing voice could've tamed a wild animal. It had the opposite effect on him. Sam was clearly smitten. He poured her a steaming cup of coffee, and Jack watched as her lips came in contact with the mug, eyes closing with apparent pleasure as she swallowed the strong brew. Sam was smiling like a simpleton. Jack had never seen him react like that to anyone. He didn't like it.

Both her kindness to the withered Sam and obvious fondness for black coffee surprised him. Jack wasn't prepared to cut her any slack. Wordlessly, Sam slid the morning paper toward her as though they'd done this many times before. She worked magic with her smile, and Sam blushed as he carried dirty dishes to the sink.

Was it possible she hadn't noticed him in the booth behind her when she sat down? *Dear God, how could she not notice?* Jack wondered. He'd thought of little else since they'd met.

"You got business here in town?" Jack was surprised when the words actually left his mouth. There was a slight hesitation before she answered. Maybe she *hadn't* known he was there.

"Uh huh," she said, opening the paper.

"Staying long?"

His peace and quiet had been disturbed since this attractive stranger walked in last night. Hair the color of well-aged cherry wood, it was tied with a ribbon of the same color. It bothered him that he noticed that detail. Met with silence, he continued to push as if he had a right to know. "What brings you to town?"

"Alice," she said, inclining her head toward the window.

Looking in that direction and seeing no one, he turned back. "Alice?"

He understood what she was doing. He'd been rude with his one-word responses when they met, and apparently she was giving as good as she got.

"Alice - my car. She and Anita take me wherever I wanna go," she said, paging through the newspaper.

"Ok, I'll bite, who's Anita?" He was beside her now, standing close enough to smell her fresh scent, wanting her to be aware of his proximity, surprised he was pressing for answers.

Her spontaneous smile lit deep emerald eyes as she took another sip of coffee. She was perfection. "My GPS. You know - Ah-Need-A address. Anita tells me where to go, Alice gets me there." Her laugh crinkled her flawless nose. She set the mug on the counter and finally made eye contact. He felt like he'd been sucker punched by what appeared to be her innocent sensuality.

"Ah, a wise ass. You still haven't answered. How long are you here for?"

"As long as it takes," she replied cryptically, unsatisfactorily, moving ever so slightly away from him.

"As long as what takes?" What was the matter with him? Why was he goading her? He'd only seen her once. He needed to get a grip. He hadn't let a woman get under his skin like this since Marcie. Just the thought of Marcie made him crazy. He threw bills on the table for the coffee that sat cold in his cup. Nodding to Sam as he left, he paused, "It's not important how long you're here, as long as you're gone soon."

Chapter Two

HOUNDS OF HELL

When the jingle of the bells stopped, Sam and I exchanged the smile of old friends. I couldn't help my burst of laughter.

"He's a friendly sort," I said with more than a touch of sarcasm. "That was almost fun."

"I ain't never seen him so rude." Sam had a rascally smile as he wiped down the counter. "He's about the finest feller I know."

By way of changing the subject, I said, "I understand you and my dad go way back?" I wasn't ready to dwell too long on Jack Franklin and the motivation behind his surly manner.

"Your pa was fresh outta college when he came up here. We both were looking for something, and he found it in your ma. She was living in Denver and passed through one day. They thought it was kismet, him being Charles and her being Charlie. I was downright heart broke when they moved outta the area 'cuz they was expecting you. Your ma didn't wanna risk the cold winters and isolation that come with being up here, so Charles took her back to Denver. The rest, as they say, is history."

"I don't remember spending any time here when I was growing up."

"Your pa finally came back to build his cabin when your ma died. We was fast friends again, as if no time had passed at all. We kept in touch over the years, but I've waited a mighty long spell to finally meet the little bundle of joy that made 'em move. I just never expected to wait all these years," he said affectionately. "I can die a happy man now. Your pa told me some of what's been going on with you. You gotta know you're safe here. Ain't gonna let nobody get near you."

"That means a lot. You make me feel like I've come home," I said, patting his hand. "Things got pretty rough for a while. One of these days we'll talk about it. In the meantime, I can't imagine a more heartfelt welcome than what you've given me. I can't believe my mom didn't want to stay."

"Don't forget, they didn't have no fancy house on a hill. They had a little cabin that blew a lotta cold air when the snows came. Easy enough for two healthy young 'uns, but it weren't no place for a baby."

"When my dad suggested I stay at his cabin and told me I could make it my escape hatch, that's what I was expecting - a not-quite-drafty large room. In my wildest dreams I couldn't have imagined what I found. What a magnificent place. I don't think I'll ever want to leave."

"That'll be all right with every one of us. I'm thinking ain't nobody gonna mind having you around." There was that wicked grin again.

"I never could figure out why he was so secretive about his *Fortress of Solitude*. He wouldn't even let me come up while it was being built."

"It was part of his healing time. They'd talked so often about coming back, and now here he was, doing it without her. It was an emotional time for him, but she sure woulda loved it."

"Wouldn't she, though? She would've changed her mind in a heartbeat about being here. I will always be sorry she wasn't able to see it."

"Seasons. Everything in its own time."

"Well, I, for one, am ready for this season. I can't wait to hide in a remote setting and find out who Callie Weston is. I've lost touch with the woman she's become because she never slows down long enough for me to get to know her."

"I know for a fact you're gonna like what you find."

WITH A THERMOS OF FRESH COFFEE AND MY NEW NIKON, I SET OFF FOR a day's adventure. Normally dressed to the nines for work, I felt totally carefree in my hiking boots, jeans, and long-sleeved tee shirt. My SUV took to the winding dirt roads with ease. The surroundings were lush and the colors were vibrant as summer was closing her final chapters. I found a trailhead close to town, parked, and headed out.

My father's familiar ring was a pleasant diversion as I looked forward to chiding him.

"Yeah, yeah, you old buzzard. How could you have kept *this* a secret?"

"Hey, sweetheart," he said with affection. "I see you made it okay?"

"Not only did I make it, I'm giving you fair warning, I may never leave."

His voice was wistful. "It does have a compelling draw, doesn't it? We were right out of college. Nederland was a place where hippies were welcomed, and we wanted to be part of the movement. But we had to work to get the money to pay for the land, then you came along and one thing led to another, and we never made it back."

"Can you imagine how much she would've loved it? It's such a work of art. It's ingenious how it fits into the landscape but still has such warmth." I was bewitched again thinking about his place. "A view over the Rockies *and* the water - hidden but accessible, great functionality, it's the *best*." I was almost self-conscious at how I was carrying on. "Can you tell I love it?"

"I'm glad. I'm pretty pleased with it myself."

"It has to be a Montgomery, right? He's too unique not to recognize his work, but how did you score *that*, and how could you have kept *that* secret from me?"

"I've known him for years. When I finally decided to build, I asked if he'd do the design if my crews did the actual work. It's his specialty, and he was glad to help."

"Wait. What rock have I been living under that this is fresh news? When I figure out where I want to spend the next phase of my life, do you think I can ask very sweetly for similar consideration?"

There was a genuine laugh. "Oh, honey, he's way past the point in his life where he might be swayed by a pretty face. But when the time comes, I'll see what I can do."

"I'll hold you to it, and I'll try to make it sooner rather than later before he keels over."

"He's got a year or two before he retires, so you've got a little time."

"Be that as it may, you may still have to kick me out after the spring thaw. I'm not sure I'll ever want to leave. Some serious heart attachment already. Good job, old man."

"Glad you like it. What did you think of Sam?"

"What a treasure he is. He's been so helpful and the Amber Rose already feels like a second home. It's got the warm leather booths and carved wooden stools, and I feel like I've always known Sam, so I'm blissfully content."

"He'll protect you with his life. We've been friends for decades."

"He told me some of your history. Stories you've never talked about. He's regaling me with your darkest secrets," I teased. "But truly, I loved hearing his tales. There was someone else there . . ."

"Yeah?"

"A guy named Jack Franklin . . . you know him?"

There was a pause before he answered. "Good man, that Jack. They don't come much finer, but he's chasing a pack of demons. Protect yourself, pun'kin. I hear he has some razor-sharp teeth."

"Oh, no worries on this end. I haven't seen the 'good man' side of him yet. And I'm coming to get away from crazy men, remember, not run into the arms of the devil himself."

I WAS ANIMATED WHEN I GOT BACK TO TOWN AND FELT LIKE A KID AT the thought of telling Sam about my first outing. The weather was holding and it was still warm. I'd taken some phenomenal shots of wildlife and scenery from the top of a hill that had been simple to climb. Until I knew the area better, I'd start with easy trips.

Several people were sitting at the counter and booths when I walked in. Sam got a huge grin and held up a cup, almost in salute, and set it at the end of the counter, motioning for me to sit there. I wasn't in a mood to relax, so I followed Sam to the back and asked if there was anything I could do to help.

"I just fixed a fresh pot. If you wanna warm up cups while I put another one on to brew, I wouldn't object."

"Sure thing," I said, loving how familiar it all felt. I was emptying the last of the coffee into a cup when I saw Jack standing there. My expression didn't change, even though my heart rate did.

I'd been wearing a heavy cloak of indifference to shield me from the crazy forces surrounding me. It had been conscious self-protection, but I could feel it falling away. Now was not the time to think about what Jack did to me, but on some level I didn't mind at all. It meant I was alive. I hadn't let my guard down enough to feel anything in so long that this instinctive enjoyment was welcome.

Playfully I said, "Take a seat, cowboy, I'll get a fresh pot." I winked as I headed to the kitchen. I wasn't sure he'd be there when I came back, but I didn't care. I felt vibrant.

"You might want to start another one, Sam. Drained this pot dry and more to go." I headed back to the dining room.

He was sitting in a booth, staring out the window.

"What brings you to town, stranger?" I teased, pouring him a cup of coffee.

His rugged smile seemed to surprise his face.

"Nothing nearly so elegant as Alice." His expression was soft. "I came in more on the Hounds of Hell."

"That musta been a rough ride. You keep 'em tied up 'round here?"

"Nah. I let 'em run free as much as possible. Hoping someone else will take 'em off my hands."

Our eyes met. Gently I said, "If you don't feed them, they'll lose their power and go looking for another lost soul to torment."

"I'm waiting for that day, little one. But they're not hanging around nearly as much as they used to."

I loved the spell his voice created, the insight he'd given without revealing anything, and his term of endearment.

"Want something to eat?"

"Sam putting you to work?"

"Nah. Had such a good day and wanted to share it, but when I came in it was busy and I offered to help. Not used to relaxing. Something I hope to learn while I'm here."

"What had you all wound up?"

"Doesn't take much for me," I laughed. "I want to become an adept photographer - of everything. I took a hike and got scenery shots and close ups of some of the fall vegetation. Helps me look at things with a different eye."

"You been over to the Carousel yet?"

"Not yet."

"Can't stay around here without knowing about the Carousel of Happiness. Took Robert twenty-six-plus years to carve the life-sized pieces and paint them. It's a work of art. I imagine it would be an unusual photo op for you."

"Then I'll make sure it's on my agenda soon."

"How about the Pioneer Inn? It used to be a hangout for Rock legends like Elton John, Billy Joel, Carole King - lots of the big names came up to record at Caribou. Not a whole lot there, but certainly a piece of the town's history to help you get a feel for the place."

"Thanks, Jack, think I'll start there. So many times in so many houses I've wished the walls could talk. Can you even imagine the stories *that* place has to tell?"

"I'd have paid good money to join in on any one of those jam sessions."

"Sounds like an interesting place. You hungry? Sam just took a meatloaf out of the oven."

"You said the magic words."

IT WAS DARK BY THE TIME I GOT HOME. I COULD SEE THE FAINT LIGHTS of the town through the expanse of glass that overlooked Barker Reservoir. Even so, the house had a sense of privacy as well as an illusion of being suspended in mid-air. If I'd searched the world for an ideal escape, I couldn't have conceived of a more perfect hideaway.

The floors looked like warm mahogany. I wondered if I laid on them if my hair would get lost in the color, and if that had been an intentional choice on my dad's part. The elegantly recessed light fixtures gave more-than-adequate illumination. Curved walls gave separation to the open flow of the rooms, and tall ceilings were obviously angled for heavy snows.

The kitchen was polished granite with a large island that had plenty of room for sitting or leaning. The Wolf stove was gleaming steel, and there was even a wine refrigerator neatly tucked under the island. He'd spared no expense. The pantry was stocked with enough food to ride out the winter. Soft towels and summer fresh sheets filled the linen closet. It was so well organized, I imagined fairies had arranged the shelves.

I poured myself a glass of wine and sat in front of an inviting fire, thinking about the surroundings. The house spoke to me, assuring me I was safe, that I could let go, that there was protection here, that I was home.

Chapter Three

AMBER ROSE

*L*ost in dancing flames that were alive with cavorting shadows, my mind drifted to when I first met Angie during our sophomore year in college. As unalike as two people can be, we hit it off immediately and were inseparable during those formative years. Not too long after graduation, Angie married Mark, a very nice but boring young man she'd met the previous year.

As Maid of Honor, I was paired with Mark's Best Man, his brother, Jason. Pleasant on the surface, not very tall but somewhat attractive with a muscular body and chiseled features surrounded by short-cropped blond hair, I had no interest in him and rebuffed his advances more times than I could count. I kept my distance. Angie kept telling me I was being unreasonable.

"Come on, Callie," said the starry-eyed young bride-to-be. "Please go out with him. He's such a nice guy. I think you'll like him a lot, and he's crazy about you."

"You know how much I love you, Ang, but you and I are looking for different things. Jason is so intense, kinda creepy intense. I don't want to get married for years yet. I want to travel and work and build a name for myself. I can't imagine Jason would be good for just a few dates, so why bother?"

"Not even for me?"

"Not even for you," I insisted. "We've had a great time planning your wedding. But it's been your fairy tale, not mine. The planning and the doing and the excitement will be over soon, and then I'm going to throw myself into my work with that same kind of determination. I don't need clinging young men messing up my plans. Besides, he told me he's looking for someone who will stay home, take care of his house, not work, and raise his kids. While I want kids someday, the thought of being tied down at this point in my life makes me swoon with hysteria."

"How can we be so different and yet so close? I'm so eager to marry Mark and start a family, I can hardly wait."

The subject of Jason came up many times over the years, and each time I remained steadfast in my insistence that I wouldn't go out with him. Angie and I stayed close, even during the birth of her two babies, but I never changed my mind about Jason - never.

It made me sick to my soul that thoughts of Angie and Jason intruded on my tranquility. There was only one car parked at the Amber Rose as I came back from a long day of dealing with business in Denver. I knew Sam's friendly face would help get rid of the frustrations and ghosts of my day.

He came from the kitchen when he heard the bell. "Well, look who's here. Glad to see you got back. Expecting a heck of a storm tomorrow."

"Hey, Sam. It looked like it might be quiet around here. Thought I'd stop and say 'hello,' see how you're doing."

"Better'n most," he said with a wink. "Coffee?"

"No, thanks. I was hoping to get a little something to eat. Got any leftovers?"

"Sure enough. You set yourself right down and I'll get something all fixed up for you." He headed to the kitchen, and a moment later the back door closed and the car outside started, its lights illuminating the darkness of the parking lot.

"Who was that?" I asked as he set down a steaming plate of Salisbury steak, mashed potatoes, and green beans.

"Want a malted to go with that?"

"Are you ignoring my question?" I teased, looking at him closely.

"What question was that?" he said, turning away, but not before I caught a blush creeping to explode above his beard.

"Well, aren't you a sly devil? And no thanks, I'll just take water."

When he returned with a tall glass of iced water, I decided not to chide him about who his ghostly visitor might've been. He'd tell me when he was ready. "Looks delicious. I need to stop going all day without eating. I get so busy I completely forget, then I'm ravenous. I'll start packing on the pounds if I'm not careful."

"That sure ain't gonna happen. You never slow down long enough for those pounds to be able to catch you."

The image of running away from Pac Man-type creatures that were chasing me made me smile, and led to another thought.

"Remember that first morning you and I talked? You told me about my mom and dad coming here, told me how they were looking for something, how they found it in each other? You mentioned you were looking for something, too. Did you ever find it?"

Sam got a faraway look. He'd been wiping the counter, a habit that must've become unconscious over the years, when finally he smiled and said, "Yeah, pun'kin, I sure did."

I was slowly eating my meal, staying quiet, hoping he'd continue.

"Back in the '60s, me and Rose was so much in love, we knew we could do anything. She had the biggest heart of anyone I ever did meet. All she wanted was to help people and to love her Sam. She was a tiny thing. Hair past her waist, it was so unruly she used to wear it in two big braids. I'd pick flowers and weave them into her hair and she'd laugh and say they made her a true flower child.

"We decided to do what a lotta our friends was doing, joined the Peace Corps. We got married in a field in Boulder before we left. Even though the times was about free love and free spirit, Rose and me loved each other. We made it legal 'cuz we wanted to be together."

I treasured listening to him. I could see Rose clearly, imagined her happily with a young Sam in a field of daisies. I didn't want to break the spell, so I waited, hoping nothing would happen to disturb his tale. A few moments later he began again, and I knew he was with her, wherever they'd gone.

"We ended up in Ecuador. We both spoke Spanish before we left so it didn't take long for us to learn the real stuff down there. We made a pact that even when we was alone, we'd speak it so we'd know it well enough to not have any trouble with the people we was there to help.

"Won't never forget the first morning she woke and was all excited because she'd dreamt in Spanish. Felt like she'd truly accomplished something. Everything about her was fresh, excited, new. It was hard to be unhappy when she was around, she was so full of life."

I'd finished eating but didn't want to move. He seemed to become conscious of where he was. He didn't say anything when he took my dishes and came back with a plate of cherry pie and a cup of coffee.

"Gave you some decaf. No sense being awake tonight."

Still I remained silent, not wanting to sidetrack him from finishing his account of what set him on his journey to this little town.

"One morning she woke and was nauseated," he continued, "and was tickled at the thought she might be pregnant. The next morning she threw up, and continued with nausea for most of the day. She wasn't hungry at all, and by the end of the day, she was real sick with a headache. In the whole time I knew her, she'd never complained about anything, so I knew she weren't feeling well.

"At the end of the third day, she started feeling better. She seemed like her old self for a day or two, but then she woke up sick again. Her whole body was sore, and her skin was a sickly yellow. She caught a glimpse of herself in the mirror and told me she would forever be my Amber Rose.

"When the doc arrived, he told us it was yellow fever and there was no medicine to get rid of it, only to make her as comfortable as possible and she'd probably get better. He pulled me aside and told me I should think about getting her to the hospital, which was hours away. By the time we got there, she was in a coma. She lived for two more days and never woke up."

My tears fell softly, a sigh catching in my throat. Sam looked at me and patted my hand. "It's been long enough now I can think of her like she used to be. Sweetest little thing God ever created. I took her body home and wandered. Didn't want to talk to nobody, didn't want people around, didn't care if I lived. After a couple of years, I ended up here – perfect place, as you're finding out, to get away from the demons that chase you.

"That's when I met your pa, and he was so good at letting me get it all out. I started to heal some, and decided this was a good place to stay. Can't tell you how much it hurt to see him and your ma leave - and how good it feels to have you here."

"I'm sorry." I hurt for him.

"It's been almost forty years now. It becomes part of what makes you who you are. But thanks for letting me tell you about my Rose. It's nice to keep her memory alive."

"I understand. I have a new appreciation for all of this," I said, sweeping my arm to encompass his place.

"Yep, she woulda loved it here. And she sure woulda loved you. Not a day goes by I don't think of her."

"Thank you for telling me. She sounds wonderful, and I love you even more than I did before."

For the second time that day, I saw Sam blush to his hairline.

"So who went out the back door earlier?" I asked. Since he had been so forthcoming about Rose, I thought maybe he'd tell me about who it was that'd been visiting him.

"Get on down the road with you now, Missy. It's late and I need to be closing up this place."

"Okay, if you're gonna be that way, I'll go. Anything I can do to help?"

"Not a darned thing. Get on now. And don't venture out tomorrow if the weather's too bad."

"Don't you know that little boys who lie a lot grow up to be weathermen? I'll believe it when I see it."

"Don't go getting all cocky on me, young 'un. It can change in the blink of an eye up here. Don't you go doin' nothin' foolish."

"Of course, sir." I went around the counter and kissed him on his cheek. "You're so special, Sam. I'm sorry it took so long, but I'm glad you're in my life now."

"Me too, honey."

NOT NEARLY AS BAD AS EXPECTED, THE 'BIG STORM' LEFT ONLY A dusting of snow. I was in the mood to explore and decided to walk to the Pioneer Inn. To the casual observer, it was probably just a hole-in-the-wall bar in a nowhere kinda town, but when you knew the history of all of the 'greats' of the '70s music era that hung out here, it took on a life of its own.

Coming in from the brightness of the snow-covered ground, my eyes had to adjust to the dim interior. I was surprised at the number of people since it was just late morning, but couldn't help smile as Frank Sinatra crooned from the jukebox to this tough-looking crowd. The rough-hewn-wood walls and booths made it a classic Colorado mountain bar. I approached the smiling waitress to introduce myself and ask if she would mind if I took a few pictures.

"Hey, guys, this here's Callie Weston," she called out loud

enough to be heard over talking patrons and music. "She's Charles' daughter. Anyone mind she gets a few shots?"

There was only a momentary silence as all eyes turned my way before the din of voices erupted again. There was laughter and suggestive comments as people went about their business.

"It's all yours, doll. Shoot away."

"Think I'll sit and let things die down so I'm not so intrusive," I said, sliding into a booth.

"Name's Candice," said the friendly server with the big hair. "Getcha something?"

"I'd love some coffee and something to eat. What do you recommend?"

"We're famous for our burgers."

"Then coffee and a burger it is."

As she walked away, I looked around the rustic interior and thought of all the life that had taken place here. I couldn't help but overhear some of the stories of the locals. More than once, the words *Bella Roja* hit my ears, but I had a feeling they intended for me to hear.

Candice came back several times and sat for a quick chitchat while we waited for food. I'd come back later when it was quieter and listen to some of her tales. This was not only how she learned her stories, but also how the locals got much of their information. Wanting to fit in, I shared what was reasonable, and noticed several people straining to hear what Candice and I were talking about.

Many of these people had a gruff exterior, much like Sam, and each had their own story that brought them here. I'd have to make this a regular stop while I was in town. Candice was a pleasant woman who'd been here over twenty-five years. She knew everyone and everything there was to know about them and had a lot of funny stories to tell. Lots of pictures and lots of laughter later, I headed home with a promise of future visits.

The walk didn't take long in the brisk mountain air. I settled in with a roaring fire and a hot cup of cocoa, and mused on the turn my life had taken recently. Sitting on the floor with legs crossed, I was happy and carefree editing my recent photos, content with the crackling flames.

Thoughts of last spring and Jason didn't intrude into my psyche as often as they once had. When I considered he would be released from jail soon, I was secure in the knowledge I was protected and safe in this little town that was close to everything but in the middle of nowhere. Even though I hadn't been here long, I was the daughter of Charles Weston. That afforded me a sort of local status that made me 'one of them.' The town was small, the locals were rough, but they took care of their own. I was out of harm's way.

Chapter Four

LOST IN THE RAIN

The darting tongues of flames in the crackling fire were mesmerizing and separated me from today's photos, throwing me into memories I wanted to forget. For years I'd been busy pursuing my career. I taught real estate law on the campus of CU Boulder, promoted my business and my father's business, sold real estate, and didn't want to be diverted too much from my path.

I'd been neglecting playtime in my life and knew I wasn't getting any younger, and part of me wanted to have a family of my own. I needed to slow down and smell the roses. Not that I didn't love what I did for a living, but my personal life was looking like a box of raisins. I was more than willing to shake it up and start rearranging priorities.

Angie called one morning in April. "Hey, sugar. Mark and I are going to The Fort this weekend. Since your birthday is coming up, we thought it would be fun to have you join us, our treat."

It'd been almost a year since we'd spent time together, and The Fort had been a place we used to go on special occasions. Feeling guilty because I'd been neglecting our friendship, I said, "I'd love to, thanks. It'll be fun to catch up."

I was furious when I showed up and Jason was sitting at the table with them. How could Angie have done this to me, and how could I have been so preoccupied as to not suspect she might try something like this? Inwardly fuming, I almost cringed as Jason stood up and kissed my cheek.

"If the mountain won't go to Mohammed, as they say . . ." He snickered, a sound that clenched my stomach. I looked at Angie and couldn't believe the Cheshire grin she wore. I didn't want to be rude because it was Mark's brother and he was a great guy, but I wasn't sure I could maintain civility for long.

I tried, truly I did. But the longer we were at dinner, the more desperate I was to leave. I wasn't sure what it was about him that made my skin crawl. Charming on the surface, not too bad to look at, why did he make me so uncomfortable? But this meeting was no different than any of the others, and if it was possible, he was even creepier than before.

Sitting around the fire outside, sipping on an after-dinner coffee, I was counting the minutes until I could leave without being obvious. We were catching up, but Jason kept rubbing my leg, touching my back. I couldn't sit any closer to Angie than I was, so when I took Jason's hand to hold it still on the seat between us, he thought I was coming on to him. He was insufferable.

Tired and no longer wanting to put up with his boorish behavior, as soon as he stepped away, I was able to excuse myself. I was getting angrier with Angie as I thought about her sneaky behavior, so when I said my good-byes, I couldn't help but wonder at the smirk that crossed her face. I was so anxious to leave that I hurried to make it to my car before Jason came back from wherever he'd gone. I was thankful the night was over.

Sometime soon I'd take the time to think about how I'd been blindsided and about how I was going to have a hard time trusting Angie again, but now I just needed to get away. As I approached, I could see in the lights of the parking lot that Jason was leaning against my car waiting for me. I wanted to scream, especially when I saw the self-satisfied grin on his face.

"Angie told me you'd gone. I was anxious to leave, too," he shared. "I knew you were feeling our chemistry. I can't wait to be alone with you."

Hiding my shock, I said as nicely as I could summon, "I'm sorry, Jason. I'm afraid you totally misread the situation. I'm utterly exhausted and anxious to get home. I have a long day ahead of me. Thank you for dinner, but I assure you, our evening is over."

The light in his eyes changed just before he roughly grabbed me and kissed me. I was surprised only momentarily. Lifting my fashionable heel, I came down as hard as possible on his foot. Stunned enough to let go, I jumped in my car and took off, watching him in my rearview mirror standing under the light.

"Crap, that was a narrow escape." I was angry and tired and wanted to shake Angie. I didn't ever want to be in the same room with that jerk again. Before I made it home, I had three text messages from him. I knew I was going to have to deal with him sooner or later, but I wasn't in the mood tonight.

This was going to put a crimp in wanting to go out with anyone again for a while. How many times did I have to tell her? What was the matter with her? I knew we had been drifting apart and I hadn't wanted to admit it, but this might be the end. Not for the first time I wondered how someone as nice as Mark could have a brother like this?

When Angie called all excited the next day to tell me how much Jason liked me and wanted to know how I felt about him, I was seriously surprised. Was she honestly that clueless? "Ang," I said as nicely as possible, "it's not ever gonna work out between us. How many times do I have to tell you that before you believe me?"

"But I saw you take his hand, Cal. I saw you holding it while we sat by the fire. You didn't look like you minded him too much then." I could hear the testiness in her voice.

"It's not at all what you thought you saw," I said, stunned. "Fact of the matter is, his hands kept traveling all over me and I was trying to hold it still between us so he would stop touching me." It wasn't my desire to be brutal, but I wanted to stop it once and for all.

"I don't like Jason, period. Not now, not ever. I don't want to have any further discussion about it. We're looking for different things and our worlds are never going to mesh. I know how much you wanted it to, but it's not going to work out."

"You couldn't be more wrong, Callie. Why would I ever want to fix my brother-in-law up with someone who would lead him on like that?"

I knew she was hurt, but I was incredulous at her response. She hadn't heard a word I said, and was definitely not being rational about the situation. I tried to bring our conversation back to some kind of normal, but she abruptly said, "Bye, Callie," and disconnected our call. Not for the first time, I wondered why we hang on to old relationships when we have long ago grown apart.

That afternoon I had an appointment with past clients who were being transferred out of state and wanted me to sell their house for them. Hopefully that would take my mind off the situation with Jason, since the preparation for my meeting would keep me busy.

But I kept thinking about Angie, and how could she have misread the situation so completely? Had I done anything at all to lead Jason on? The only thing I was guilty of was staying as long as I had. I needed to shake it off and get on with my day.

My assistant is second to none. Marge has been with me from the start of my career. I was young but enthusiastic when I got my real estate license. I knew the business well, learning from the best.

My dad was a high-end home builder who had taken me under his wing at a young age, and I felt confident I knew not only houses, but dealt well with people as they embarked on what was usually an emotion-filled time in their life - purchasing or selling a home. Marge had been a 'gift' from my dad when I was still green behind the ears. She was a gem and we were a dynamic team. We had been together long enough that we worked comfortably together. So when I walked into the office that day, I knew Marge had something on her mind.

"What is it?" I asked with a grin.

"Jason Stevens . . . how did you end up seeing him again?"

"What a nightmare. He is such a cretin, and I'm afraid Angie's not too far behind."

Marge slid the stack of messages across the desk, "Well, he obviously didn't agree with you. He's called six times this morning."

"Will he go away if I ignore him?" I teased. "I can't imagine dealing with him again, but I guess I'm gonna have to be even more blunt and tell him what he obviously didn't understand with the point of my heel."

Laughing, I headed into my office to get on with the business of my day. Marge followed, wanting all the details. Marge's kids were grown, and she loved to not only hear my stories, but protected me like a mother hen. Few were as competent or as loyal.

"He's gonna be trouble, a real thorn." She shook her head. "You need to deal with him and get rid of him as fast as you can."

Meeting her gaze, I gave her words some thought.

"Don't look at me in that maternal tone," I said, winking. "Fact of the matter is, it makes me angry that someone who's as crass as Jason has already commanded this much attention. Can we forget about him for today and get to work on the Stewart's file? Let's not waste any more time until I can figure out how to best to approach it."

She scowled like she didn't want to let it go. "That's fine for now, but this won't be swept under the rug as easily as you think. He's off balance," she said ominously as she headed back to her desk.

WHY WAS I DWELLING ON IT AGAIN? WHY WAS I GIVING THIS PSYCHO space in my head? I packed my computer, bundled up in a hooded coat, and headed off to my favorite hangout. I'd show Sam the pictures I'd taken and untangle myself from the web I'd woven around me this afternoon. I didn't want Jason to ever have power in my life again.

Walking in the back door, my heart skipped a beat when I heard Sam talking. I was warming to the mercurial stranger known as Jack Franklin, and I wasn't disappointed he was there. "Hey, guys," I said, hanging up the last of my warm winter coverings.

Both of them turned at the sound of my voice. Sam took my computer and set it on the counter. "Hey, pun'kin. It was crazy around here earlier, but seeing's how it's quiet right now, Jack and me was just talking about starting a game of checkers or something."

Jack winked as I caught a glimpse of him over Sam's shoulder, causing a flutter in the vicinity of the center of my chest. "Before you do that, I'd love to show you the pictures I took at the Pioneer Inn this morning. I did some artsy things, and I want to share them with someone."

Like a tolerant sibling, Jack pulled out a stool for me while Sam came out with the ever-faithful mug of coffee. Forty-five minutes passed with each of them sharing stories about the people in my photos, and how the Pioneer Inn had become the 'home away from home' for world-famous recording artists who came to Caribou Ranch to cut albums at a time when long-haired hippie types weren't welcome in many establishments. They gave me a whole new appreciation for some of the images I'd captured. I was over-flowing with thankfulness for their genuine appreciation and feed-back to my morning's work.

"You two are the best," I said, packing up my computer. "Thanks for your indulgence."

"Did you walk down?" Jack asked.

"Yeah, it doesn't take too long and it's good exercise. I don't mind at all."

"Well, the sun is going down and I'm heading home, so I'll give you a lift."

"Thanks, but that's not necessary," I said, slipping on my gloves.

"It may not be necessary, but it's gonna happen," Sam said.

Looking from one to the other, I accepted the inevitable. I didn't want to be overly dramatic in my refusal, but there were many reasons I didn't want to be in the small confines of a car with this man who jumbled my senses. If my mantra had become that I wasn't going to let the past have control over my future, I opted to accept his offer with grace.

"Thank you, Jack. I'd appreciate that."

Giving each other a questioning look, Sam said, "That weren't at all what I was expecting outta our feisty one. Watch your back, son."

We all laughed as Jack picked up my computer and set it by the front seat in his Land Cruiser.

"Your chariot awaits," he said with a sweep of his hand.

"Thank you ever so much, gallant sir," I said with a slight curtsy.

We drove the short distance in silence. As he pulled into the drive, Jack turned and said softly, "You did a remarkable job with your photos from this morning. Impressive."

It seemed like huge praise coming from him, and I blushed as I thanked him for the compliment and the ride. As he started to open his car door to get out, I said, louder than intended, "*Don't!*"

"I was merely going to make sure you made it into the house safely," he said quietly.

"Thank you, but this is fine. If it makes you feel better, you can make sure I get into the house, but no need for you to get out of the car. I'll flash the light when the door is locked."

I rushed to get the front door open and get inside before he could challenge my request. I flashed the light to let him know I was in safely, and wondered at my conflicting emotions as I leaned against the front door. He definitely disturbed my peace of mind.

WEEKS PASSED AND I SETTLED INTO A PLEASANT ROUTINE. MY DAYS

were filled with photography, editing, writing guest articles for national Realtor publications, and addressing whatever issues Marge needed help with at the office.

What a morning this had been. The hike up the hill had allowed me to get the photos I wanted and then some. I carried a small rain poncho in my camera bag, and when the brief rains started to fall softly, I put it on and continued with my shots. It had not been enough to dampen my spirits nor the excitement of capturing my surroundings. Few places I'd seen were more breathtaking than sitting on the side of this mountain with the sun reflecting off the water and a breeze churning whitecaps. The warm colors of autumn were fading, but there was still beauty in the stark contrasts around me. I was totally lost in the splendor of it, and knew completely that I loved the sense of not being able to be found by anyone.

Scrambling to get to level ground, I froze when the bobcat crossed my path. Its feline grace thrilled me. I had my camera ready, and the seemingly unaware creature appeared to be posing. I knew I was getting fabulous shots, and lost myself in the incredible beauty of nature and landscape.

Unaware of how long I'd been shooting, I was shocked when a lightning bolt hit nearby, exploding a rock into hundreds of fragments. I became conscious that it was raining and I was freezing. A cold front was coming in rapidly over the mountain. Typical Colorado weather – if you don't like it, so the expression goes, wait five minutes and it'll change. That seemed to be even truer at this higher elevation.

I could hear the car speeding up the winding road as I moved as fast as my freezing limbs would allow. I scrambled to get across the dirt road before whoever it was came around the blind curve. The mud-splattered Jeep burst around the bend. How could the driver possibly see anything out of the filthy windshield? As it sped up the road, it scattered mud and gravel everywhere, leaving me looking as though I'd been doused with a melted Snickers.

Catching my breath from the thick, cold mess covering me, a

second vehicle came around the corner at a more sedate speed. I inched closer to a large boulder on the edge of the road to make sure I was well out of the way and would be no distraction to the driver. Spotting me standing there, Jack slowed and pulled over.

"Lost?" he called as his window rolled down. "What in the world happened to you?" He pulled as far as he could to the side of the narrow road. I hadn't said a word, just stood there looking at him. He had to be well over six feet tall, my jumbled brain registered as he came around to the front of his car.

"Cat got your tongue?" he seemed to purr.

He looked me up and down, from my filthy boots to my matted hair, and his smile grew even bigger. At first I wanted to be angry he would find my predicament so amusing. But the fact of the matter was, I was standing in the middle of nowhere, freezing, covered in mud, storm coming in, and in an utterly ridiculous situation. I couldn't imagine how truly ratty I must look.

The rain started again, igniting laughter. The more I laughed, the bigger his smile became, until we were standing in the cold with the wind howling, laughing, both of us getting wet.

"Hurry," he called above the rising wind. "We're on this corner and it'll be dangerous to anyone else coming up the mountain, especially in this weather."

He tossed my camera bag onto the back seat of his car, opened the passenger door, and motioned for me to get in. Mortified, I stood looking at him, noticing for the first time he was dressed in a suit. I refused.

"No way will I get in your car in my condition. Thank you for the offer, but . . . no way."

He took a step closer. "The upholstery's seen worse. Get in." Somewhere along the way I wondered if his cheeks were red from the biting wind or if his blood was pulsing like mine. Where had my brains gone? Was it the cold confusing me? I couldn't think with him standing this close, our eyes locked. His proximity took my breath away, and his spell settled around me like the encroaching fog.

In what felt like a time warp, I was surprised when his voice gentled and brought me back to reality. "Get in, little one."

Glad my face was muddy so he couldn't see me blush, I remembered my predicament. Standing on a cold cliff with this unusual man, covered from head to toe in mud, not only were we in a dangerous position, but he now had my camera equipment captive in his car. He guided me to the open door. There was a blanket on the seat so I could relax that I might do irreparable damage. The heater immediately began to penetrate my consciousness. My teeth started chattering in earnest as I leaned forward so as not to have more contact with the seat than necessary.

He pulled a jacket from the back and put it around my shoulders. "Wrap up in that and don't argue," he scowled. He pulled the coat under my chin. Our eyes met, and he ran his thumb over my drying, muddy cheek. "Cheap facial," he smiled as I tried to break the spell his soft touch had spun in our enclosed warmth. The Mercedes was warm, but I was still shaking. When he put the car in gear, I was able to take a breath.

"Home in two minutes, ma'am," he said as he expertly maneuvered the car around the muddy corners and curves.

Damn him. I could handle the indifference, I could handle the sarcasm, I could even handle the teasing. What I couldn't handle was his tender concern.

"Rather nice for mountain driving," I stuttered.

"I had an appointment in Denver. This is my cruise ship." His slight smile was surprisingly pleasant.

Shocked at how much I was shivering, it took an effort for me to mumble the words, "I must have been out there longer than I thought."

"What were you *thinking* being up there without a coat? Are you looking for trouble?"

"It was so perfect when I left. I had on boots and long sleeves. When the first shower hit, I threw on my rain slicker. When the sun came out again, I repacked it in my case. I started back some time ago, but got sidetracked by a bobcat with a luxurious coat. He wanted to pose for me."

I could see his jaw working, so I was surprised when his words were gentle. "Bobcats normally won't attack unless provoked, but rather than taking pictures, you would've been a lot safer backing away slowly, ready to throw a rock. The weather changes in the blink of an eye, and a moderate day turns to crap in no time. There aren't many afternoons it doesn't rain here, and blue skies give way to frozen shards in a hurry."

He wasn't being condescending. In fact, he sounded like he was trying to be solicitous. His voice was tender, and I was furious with myself when I felt tears sting my eyes. "I'm not a novice to the elements. Truth be told, I'm much more mortified that you found me like this."

He looked surprised. "How'd you get so muddy?" Did he know I was on the brink of tears and that's why he gentled his question? Or was it the chattering teeth that had him feeling sorry for me?

"As I was crossing the road, an old Jeep came hell bent around the curve. He never saw me, but the mud from his tires took perfect aim." I tried to smile, but could feel the mud cracking.

"Hank can't seem to take these hairpins at a reasonable speed. One of these days he's gonna hurt himself. Or worse yet, someone else."

"If you'll let me off before the turn in, I can make it from there."

Ignoring me, he continued down the long drive. Without a word, he parked the car and leaned into the back to retrieve my camera equipment. He opened my car door, held out his hand and said, "Give me the key."

Not about to argue, I dug into my mud-encrusted jean pocket, my icy hands still shaking as I handed it to him. Feeling like a child, I followed his strides that were so much longer than mine, up the stone path to the side door. By the time I entered the house, the steaming water was running in the guest-room bath.

"Get out of your clothes and in the shower."

"Yeah, right," I said under my breath, trying to get my lips to move properly.

He stopped in his tracks and glared. It was immediately obvious which one of us would win this argument, and he wasn't going to take 'no' for an answer.

"I'll get some dry clothes and leave them inside the door. You better be under the water by the time I get back or I'll put you there myself."

The balmy stream sluiced over my freezing body, and the idea of him carrying me to the shower made me shiver in a different way. Feeling seeped back into my limbs, and the parts that weren't being touched by the warm spray were being warmed by my thoughts.

The door opened a few minutes later. As he put fresh clothes on the counter, our eyes met in the mirror. If it was possible to be frozen in a hot cascade of water, I was. He broke eye contact and closed the door softly. The spell was broken, but my stability was off-center.

The smell of bacon warred with the soft scent of lotion as I applied it to my warmed body. Imagining his hands on those parts was enough to have me rushing to get my clothes on. I wouldn't allow myself to be vulnerable. Wasn't I long past being susceptible like an infatuated teenager? What was wrong with me? Morning coffee and toast had worn off several hours earlier, and the smells emanating from the kitchen had my stomach rumbling.

"I won't say anything about making yourself at home," I said, trying not to sound ungrateful.

"I know my way around the kitchen. Thought you might be hungry," he said over his shoulder. He had taken off his jacket and rolled up his sleeves.

I was surprised at his thoughtfulness. Rugged, hard, obviously capable, it was even stranger to know he had spent time in this kitchen with my father. It had never been discussed, but it was a mental shift thinking they might actually have a relationship.

"So you're friends with my dad?" Oh, was I curious.

He hesitated before answering. "We've spent a few hours together," he said noncommittally. "Anytime you get people together in a town like this, everyone tends to know everyone else."

Any further questions would be saved for a time when I could ask my dad directly. I wasn't sure I wanted to know that my father and this man to whom I was so violently attracted might be more than passing acquaintances.

Chapter Five

GRIZ

*A*s I crawled into bed that night, I thought of my earlier encounter with Jack. He was tough but gentle, kind but nobody's fool. Even with all his gruffness, he was hauntingly appealing. Unlike Jason. No matter how many times Angie brought up the name of her brother-in-law, there was nothing that would induce me to change my mind about going out with him. I couldn't stand him, and that became more pronounced over time. He, unfortunately, had other ideas.

Nothing seemed to convince Angie to back off. No words seemed to be strong enough. It didn't make sense. Angie knew me. She knew I wasn't coy or evasive. She'd often told me that one of the things she loved most about me was my brutal honesty, so telling her how much I disliked Jason should have come as no surprise that I meant what I said.

She kept throwing him at me, kept encouraging him to pursue me. She never heard a word, the primary one being "no." *He* certainly never heard me. The more I said "no," the more he thought I was playing hard to get.

There was never a time I wasn't straightforward with him. It even became a game to see how harsh I could be, but

36

nothing made him go away. Over and over I'd tell him I didn't like him, that I didn't want to see him, that I wanted him to stop calling, to stop showing up unannounced, to just stop.

A narcissist with anger issues, I came to understand he was a moral sociopath. Over time I thought of him as a terrorist who had focused not on a group, but on me. Often I thought I was losing my mind. All of the things that happened that I knew had happened but wasn't sure had happened and couldn't prove to anyone had happened - it was insanity. Sometimes I believed it must be me who was crazy.

Several times I came home and something would be out of place. Not enough to be positive it was different, but enough I questioned myself. The day I came home and found all my under-wear folded perfectly in the drawer in color order, I knew without a doubt I wasn't crazy. When I saw a pair of panties and a matching bra lying neatly on my bed, I called a locksmith and had the locks changed.

It made me sick to my stomach the next day when I received flowers at work, and the middle one was dead. The apology card attached told me how sorry he was if he'd frightened me. I threw them in the garbage, but not before taking a picture.

I blocked his number when he started faxing me apologies. That pissed him off, so he mailed me daily notes. Sometimes I'd receive ten in a day, never anything outright threatening, but always enough that I lived in fear.

After a few days, I stopped reading them because he wasn't going to incriminate himself, but I kept them all in a file. Their sheer volume was enough to be a disturbance.

I LOVED THAT TIME IN THE MORNING BETWEEN MY BRAIN WAKING AND my body following suit, what I thought of as my 'twilight' time. Lying in bed thinking about the day ahead, contemplating the issues of life, or remembering good things, I was tired of thoughts of the past intruding.

But this morning it wasn't the past that had me so restless. Jack had spent the night with me, at least in my dreams. Rather than relaxing, I'd head to the Amber Rose and talk to Sam, listen to some stories, get out and take pictures. Anything to get away from the intimacy Jack had woven yesterday when he'd taken such good care of me, fed me, lit a fire, wrapped me in a blanket on the couch, done the dishes, then slipped away when I dozed.

Coming quietly through the back door of the Amber Rose, I was surprised to see Jack leaning against the counter talking to Sam as I came through the kitchen. Gone was the intimate stranger who cooked for me yesterday. Here was the Jack that was all too familiar - eyes cold as midnight, no facial reaction, apparent indifference.

Sam turned when he saw Jack's expression and grinned ear to ear as he placed a bristly kiss on my cheek.

"I was wondering when you'd get yourself down here to see ol' Sam."

I turned to give Jack a pleasant greeting, but he was already throwing money on the counter. "Catch you later, Sam, Callie," he said as the bell jangled.

I was stung by his reaction. Solicitous yesterday, an indifferent stranger today.

"You sure do seem to rile him up," Sam snickered as he pulled out a mug and a pot of coffee. "Love seeing ol' Jack Franklin ruffled by a little slip of a thing."

The bells rang again when one of the locals came in, and Sam introduced me to Griz. We exchanged small talk. "Ah, you must be the *Bella Roja* that's causing such a ruckus around town," Griz said. "But I'm sorry to have interrupted. I need to ask your advice about something, Sam. I'll come back when you're alone."

"No problem at all," I offered. "I haven't read the paper yet, so I'll sit over here and let you two talk business."

Ten minutes later I interrupted softy. "I'm sorry. It was hard not to overhear your conversation." Sam smiled as I apologized again.

"I happen to have some knowledge about how to fix your problem."

Griz looked at me somewhat dismissively until Sam explained I was Charles Weston's daughter. His whole attitude changed. "Maybe you're not so much of a flatlander after all."

"I'm sorry to hear about your aunt's passing," I said. "If you truly don't ever want to live in the house she left you, and you don't want to make the trip to Montana to take care of the details, I have a friend who's an agent there and can handle the particulars for you. She can take care of the Title transfer into your name, get the house ready for putting it on the market, take care of the showings, and transfer the money into your bank account when it's sold."

"That would be very helpful, ma'am. I'm not able to make the trip, and I had no idea how to even start to figure it out."

"Everything can be handled electronically these days, and I'd be more than happy to take care of your end of things down here. It's no trouble at all. I do this kind of thing every day."

After getting the details, I made a few phone calls and put him in touch with the right people. I contacted Marge and made sure she would follow up with him. While the sun was high and the air had some warmth left, I headed out to explore.

"Can't thank you enough, Miss. I'm beholden to you. You ever need anything, you come find Griz. I won't forget."

"Glad I could help. No trouble at all."

When I got home later that afternoon, Jack's car was in the driveway, but he wasn't in it. Feeling foolish as my heart raced, I came in the front door and stopped as I saw him looking out over the reservoir.

"To what do I owe the pleasure?" I tried for nonchalance but it came out too breathy. I'd known him for months and it still took my breath away every time I saw him.

"I keep an eye on the place for Charles when he's not around. I'll try to break the habit while you're here." He continued to stand with his back toward me, not moving. "How long is that gonna be?" he asked quietly.

I wasn't sure I understood the question, so I didn't answer.

"How long you staying, little one?" His endearment made my heart dance. I sat down on the polished rocks of the hearth, trying to gather my composure.

"At five foot eight, I'm hardly little." I was working on casual. I wasn't sure how to get there.

"A few more months, at least," I finally replied. "I plan on riding out the winter here. I have competent staff taking care of my business and I shouldn't have to make the trip to town too often. Why?" I asked as softly as I could, not wanting to break the spell surrounding us as the sunset turned the sky crimson and gave an eerie glow to the room.

"I heard what you did for Griz today. I came to say thank you."

"No thanks necessary. It was within my power to fix his problem easily, and I was happy to help. It's important to me to fit in as much as possible."

His shoulders lost their rigidity as he leaned his head against the window. As though he thought better of it, he came and stood in front of me, not saying a word, just looking at me broodingly.

"Can't imagine that will bode well for either of us," he said as he took my hand and helped me to my feet. We stood with only breath between us, not talking, absorbing the moment, each other.

Swimming in the sea of his blue eyes, the setting sun was creating an aura of enchantment. I wanted him to kiss me but didn't want the moment to end. When he finally did, the world stopped. Wait, did I think it stopped? Then why was it spinning so frantically out of control?

His kisses were tantalizing, unlike any I'd known. I'd read about this feeling, but until this moment, didn't know it truly existed.

"I could do this for hours," I said breathlessly, not wanting to stop. Again his lips were on mine. He seemed to absorb me into his being. I was glad his arms were around me so I didn't fall. As he broke the kiss, we stood staring at each other.

"Dear God, a freight train would've done less damage," he said. He made sure I was steady on my feet, then was gone.

Every fiber of my being was alive in a new and different way. I have no idea how long I stood there willing my body to move. I took the disc out of my camera and tried editing photos. My mind wouldn't focus on anything but his lips, his soft, delectable lips. After a simple dinner and a luxurious bath in a tub like a forest wonderland, I was surprised how tired I was.

The next morning I awoke restless again, wanting to see Jack, wanting to repeat the experience, wanting to know what that had been about. I headed to the Amber Rose. Maybe I could get Sam to tell me things about my mysterious stranger.

THERE WERE CUSTOMERS WHEN I CAME IN. SAM WAS BUSY, SO I HELPED out as best I could, running orders, pouring coffee, cleaning tables. After the crowd left, Sam slid a mug toward me and filled it with his fresh brew.

"Haven't seen it that busy in here since summer. I have someone who helps out in the season, but we don't usually have too much traffic up here in the winter. Sure appreciate you helping me out, pun'kin."

"Pun'kin," I said wistfully. "That's what my dad calls me. When I was a kid, my hair was kinda that color. It defined me - red hair and freckles. The older I get, the darker the color gets and the freckles are pretty much gone, thank goodness, but I love the name. It's such a term of endearment. Thanks, Sam," I said genuinely. "Did you talk to my dad much over the years?"

"Often enough. He always called you 'pun'kin' and had such nice things to say about you, I always felt like I knew you. But Charles and I, no matter how much time went by, we could always pick up right where we left off. Once your ma died, God rest her soul, he spent a lot more time up here."

"I keep thinking about how some people change. Keep thinking about how close we can be to someone for so long, then all of a sudden it's like you don't even know them. I'm glad you and my dad stayed close."

"You talking about some scoundrel that hurt you?" Sam's protective nature was showing.

"No," I said, smiling absently. "We get close to people, we share souls with them, we think we know who they are. I was close with my college roommate for twelve years. Now I wonder if I even knew her, or what it was about her I liked. I wouldn't want to have a cuppa coffee with her these days. Makes me sad. We connected on so many levels. We loved each other. There wasn't anything we didn't share. We told each other things no other human would ever know about us. Now we're polite strangers, and not even so much polite.

"I've been trying to figure out if it's time that changes us, circumstance, or we just grow apart? Was it me that failed the relationship? Are people just supposed to be in our lives for a season? Could I not have known who she truly was, or did other people's influence change her? How can you love someone like that and then look at them as though you've never seen them, never known them?"

I touched Sam's hand and chuckled. "Seems like it's been so long since I've had time to myself. Being up here alone, out of the rat race, is definitely helping me think about things I haven't slowed down long enough to think about before. My dad would say this is a time that's gonna define me."

"Or we grow up and find that most people can't be trusted," Jack said cynically from the booth behind me.

When had he slipped in, and how could I not have noticed? But I was quick to respond. "Is that fair, Jack? I don't know your story. I don't know what brought you to this little settlement. But

I *do* know you wouldn't be here if there wasn't a whole lotta trust between you and most of the people you know here."

I heard Sam chuckle behind me and knew I had Jack's attention. I could even form a rational thought in spite of the eye contact. "I don't know much about you at all, but as sure as I'm standing here, I know that trust is important to you. I'd even imagine it has a lot to do with why you live here – because you know the people here can be trusted. A spade is a spade all the way around, and you know that even if you don't agree with someone, they're shooting straight from the hip."

Sam almost cackled, "She's not only candy to the ol' eyeballs, she's a dang smart little spitfire as well."

Jack didn't break eye contact when he replied, "Most women don't know the meaning of trustworthy. Best to avoid letting them get close enough to find that out."

At first I was stung by his blanket assessment. Then my heart just hurt for whoever it was who blinded him into believing that and making him callous.

"Whoever she was, she's not worth giving up on life for. We all make mistakes in judgment. Sometimes we trust where we shouldn't." My voice got softer. I wanted him to listen to what I was saying.

"Sometimes, if we're lucky enough, we grow up and wonder, 'What the hell was I thinking?' For the most part, people are good. You have a goldmine of good people around you, which I'm sure you realize. Some of them are gonna be women, most of them are not out for blood."

He was looking in my direction, but he'd gone somewhere else. When his eyes met mine again, it was as though he physically took my face and held me immobile. "I repeat, best to avoid letting them get close enough to find out."

After a few heartbeats, without breaking eye contact, I replied, "I hear what you're saying. I don't agree with you, but I do hear you, and it's duly noted."

I turned back to Sam, not wanting to analyze the crazy thing that had just happened between us. Time enough for that later.

Sam was looking back and forth between Jack and me with his ever-present wicked grin. "Your Pa coming up any time soon?" he asked, breaking the tension.

"Only if I invite him," I replied cheekily. "How's *that* for a good deal? I get his place, and he doesn't get to visit unless I say so."

The bell on the door jingled, and when I looked, Jack had walked out. My eyes met Sam's. There was understanding in them, humor as well. But I didn't want to talk about what was happening. I wanted to think about it when I was alone, think about what was going on. Jack was warning me away, but why?

"Whenever you wanna talk, you know where to find me," Sam said gently.

Kissing him on the cheek, I whispered, "Thanks, Sam, I know."

Chapter Six

FROZEN DEAD GUY DAYS

Over the weeks I'd been welcomed by many of the people of this tiny town. Being the daughter of Charles Weston gave me entree and a certain kind of acceptance not normally afforded to strangers. I didn't mind the stares, knowing there was no threat in them, only friendly appreciation for someone different than what they were used to.

Bella Roja was a term I heard often as I explored, but it took my breath away when I heard it coming from Jack's lips as we ran into each other at the Post Office.

"You have lunch yet?" he asked.

"No. I left the house early and didn't know it was that late. I write notes to my clients when I'm sitting in front of a quiet fire in the evenings, so I came over to get stamps."

"Can I buy you lunch?"

As many times as we'd talked, my heart still did a somersault when we made eye contact. He had a zip line to my soul.

"I'd like that, thank you."

Settling into a little diner and placing our order, Jack became as talkative as I'd seen him, peppering me with questions. Never one to use a few words when a story would work, I got carried away in my response when he asked about my job.

"For as long as I can remember, my dad has been a builder in the Denver/Boulder area. As a very little girl, mom would take me to job sites so she could visit or help as dad got his business off the ground. On those days, she'd bring things to keep me occupied, but I'd always find my way to a hammer or screwdriver. While other little girls were getting dolls for Christmas, I wanted tools."

The waitress set our food on the table. "Go on," he said.

"One of my fondest memories is my first real toolbox for my tenth birthday. There've been many additions to it over the years, but I still have the core set I got twenty years ago, and I rarely use them without remembering my initial joy.

"So it wasn't a surprise to anyone when I chose a profession that had something to do with houses. I got my real estate license before I turned twenty, and for over a decade I've worked as an agent in Denver, first with my dad, then branching out on my own."

"I remember your dad mentioning some kind of award you won last year. He was over-the-moon proud."

Blushing, I said, "Ah, I've been driven for so many years. Last year I was selected for a National award they give to up-and-coming agents under the age of thirty. He *was* proud. I've done nothing but work around the clock for years. I worked hard to establish a solid reputation. One morning I woke up and realized I'd stopped living somewhere along the way. I definitely needed a break."

"Lotsa people would think this little backwater town wasn't a whole lotta living," he said, as if asking a question.

"Are you kidding? There's more life in this place than I've seen in forever. People are real. *You* get to make the choice about whether or not you want to engage. I love it here."

"You're an unusual woman, Callie Weston. A little hurricane of fresh air," he winked as he paid the tab.

THE WEATHER STAYED WARM FOR THE NEXT MONTH OR SO. THERE weren't many days I didn't visit the Amber Rose, there weren't many times I went in when Jack wasn't there. Sometimes his conversations with Sam would end abruptly when he'd see me, sometimes Jack would ask me a question and involve me in whatever it was they were talking about. One morning while Jack and I sat at the counter talking to Sam, some out-of-towners wandered in.

"You're welcome to sit wherever you want," said Sam in a friendly manner, coming around the counter to hand them menus, "just so long as there ain't nobody else in the seat."

I'd heard him say it half dozen times but it still made me laugh. Jack and I exchanged a playful glance. I loved it here. No wonder my dad couldn't wait to visit at every opportunity.

Jack got up to pour himself another cup of coffee and poured me some as well.

"You from around here?" one of the customers asked.

"I am now," I replied.

"We've heard this town has Frozen Dead Guy Days. When does that happen?"

"Not until March, but it's only the people from out-of-town that enjoy it. The locals dread it because it's nothing but a drunken brawl for three full days," I said derisively.

"People move up here because of the beauty of it, to get away from city life, to live in peace. In one weekend, thousands of people descend on this remote town, people who don't care about the destruction they're causing, and then they're gone. It takes weeks to clean up the mess of their carelessness."

I hadn't meant to be rude, but I did seem to have silenced their questions. They hid behind their menus.

"Well said," Jack said quietly, resting his hand on my knee. "You ever been here during Frozen Dead Guy Days?"

I could feel the heat of his hand warming the knee of my jeans. I stared at it. He must've become conscious of the familiarity, because he smiled and picked up his coffee, breaking the magical moment.

"I've never been, but it doesn't sound like a good time to me," I said, looking out the window into town.

"It's not usually," Jack explained. "They make it to the neighborhood where the Tuff Shed is where Grandpa's body is on ice, God rest his soul," he said teasingly. "But he's been frozen and thawed so many times, no one wants to see him. It's more of a ritual than anything else."

"Sounds so inviting." I turned back toward him.

"Maybe we can have work to do in Denver or Boulder that weekend," Jack said suggestively. "They don't usually make it near the houses. After all this time, Sam has his own system for taking care of things, so I make myself as scarce as possible."

The thought of spending a weekend in Denver or Boulder with Jack was somehow delectable. He must have recognized he was sapping my thought processes.

"One of your most admirable traits, and one I very much appreciate, is not only are your words honest, but your face is expressive. It's refreshing . . . and rare. Makes it easy to know what you're thinking," he cajoled.

"Here's how I feel about that," I said reflectively. "I'm diplomatic when I need to be, but above all else, I demand honesty. It doesn't matter the subject, it doesn't matter how tragic it is, how hurtful it might be, how much someone thinks I don't want to hear it, none of it matters as long as we're dealing with the truth. It's too hard to play the game when there are only fifty cards in the deck and you don't know which ones are missing. Real easy to get blindsided that way."

He looked at me for a moment. "You're an interesting woman. It doesn't feel like innocence or naiveté, but it's refreshing." When he touched my cheek, it brought me an inordinate amount of pleasure.

"You keep me on my toes, Jack Franklin. I like you."

"Ditto, angel, ditto," he said as he paid his tab and waved to Sam as he left. This time, however, his eyes met mine as he opened the door. This time, he smiled and winked. This time, my heart sang a little song at what had just happened.

"I could get used to this life, Sam," I said distantly. Sam, of course, just smiled wickedly.

WAS IT INTENTIONAL THAT WE MET THE NEXT MORNING AT SAM'S PLACE for coffee? Were we circling the attraction without acknowledging it?

"Gonna be a full moon tonight," Sam said as he poured coffee for both of us. "Think I'll shut down early. People seem to lose their minds during the full moon at this elevation. You two looking for breakfast?" he asked, looking between us.

"I sure could use some of your pancakes with a whole pile of bacon," Jack said.

"I'll take some oatmeal when you get around to it. As a matter of fact, why don't I grab it myself?" I said, hopping down from the stool.

"Don't even think about it. Y'all set there and I'll be right back."

A couple came in and sat at one of the booths. I handed them menus and told them I'd be happy to take their order when they were ready.

Jack smiled, "Do you ever sit still?"

"Be nice to me, Jack. Don't forget, you genuinely like me under that tough exterior of yours."

We could hear the conversation of the couple behind us. She said insistently, "Don't stumble over something that's behind you, Paul. It's not worth it, and it'll ruin our time together."

Jack and I looked at each other and nodded in agreement.

He looked me full in the face and said, "How about you? What are you stumbling over?"

It was a thought-provoking question. As I met his eyes, the lady said, "You can take our order now, Miss."

"Certainly," I said, smiling at my reprieve.

After pouring them coffee, I headed to the back and gave Sam their order. I took my seat next to Jack. He pierced me with his dagger gaze.

"You didn't think you were gonna get off that easily, did you? Spill it. What are you running from? What brought you to leave everything behind and hide here for a few months? Nasty breakup with a boyfriend?"

I laughed out loud, "Hardly that." I moved away emotionally from the subject. He must have sensed it.

"I'm no threat to your balance," he said. "You like honesty, then let's start our day with it. What makes Callie Weston tick? What happened to her that drove her to hide in the mountains with nothing familiar around her?"

"Well, *that's* not true, Jack. Dad's place was familiar the moment I walked through the doors. There's an architect I'm totally enamored with," I said, drifting off to my fantasy home. "For years I have called him 'my architect.' Dad's little cabin in the woods up here reeks of a Montgomery, so when I walked in, I felt like I'd come home."

"You friends with this Montgomery?" Jack asked, sounding jealous.

"Oh, no. I've just seen his work and it pulls at every fiber of my being. I always figured one of these days I would have him build me a home. I thought now would be a good time, but no one seems to know where he is."

"You're a smart cookie, you'll track him down if you wanna find him," Sam said from behind the counter.

"Well, thanks, Sam. I just might do that."

Turning back to Jack, I finished my thought, "I also knew Sam immediately, even though we'd never met. He was like coming home." I winked at Sam. His blush turned him a bright red. "So I wasn't completely alone. I wasn't completely thrown to the wolf."

"You mean wolves?"

"No, I said what I meant - wolf."

He threw back his head and his laugh was a balm to my soul.

"That's a sound that makes my heart happy. You should do it more often."

He stilled. "Don't change the subject. You're not going anywhere until you tell us your story." He nodded toward Sam who was watching me intently.

"Don't push her too hard, Jack. Can't you see she's fragile?"

"What is it with you two?" I asked, trying to sound offended. "Do I look like there's anything fragile about me? I've been helping my dad frame and hang drywall and lay flooring and shingle a roof since I was a kid. I'm not something to be pampered."

"Just because you can do all them things don't mean you can't be pampered. Ain't that right, Jack?" he winked as he went to offer more coffee to his customers.

"Come on. Spill it."

"Be nice to me, Jack, I'm fragile." He didn't say a word as I traveled back to early spring, back to the time when I was going to have to be cruelly honest with Jason and knew it would forever end my relationship with Angie. I no longer cared.

"Sometimes I wish I had a crystal ball to know what was around the corner. It would've made this so much easier. But then it's probably best not to know, huh?"

I told Jack and Sam about the events leading up to the fateful night, about my friendship with Angie, about the things Jason had done that caused the fear in me, and about my resolve to not let those events take over my mind or my life.

Jack's jaw was working. "What does he do for a living?"

"Engineer. No shock there, huh? Mr. Personality himself," I laughed to try to break his focus.

Jack's fist was clenching. I took his hand and rubbed it with my thumbs. Sam slammed a large mug on the counter.

"I'm safe now, guys. Nobody can hurt me here, right? I have you two to protect me." I tried to lighten the mood.

"Get on with your story or I might have to break something," Sam said through gritted teeth.

"Jason was waiting for me at my door when I got home one

night. When I told him to leave, he shoved me against the door with an elbow to my neck. He didn't have a weapon, but he was a bodybuilder and I was no match for his strength. I wanted to calm him so I could get inside, but I had to say the words, had to actually tell him never to come back. It was something I knew the police would ask.

"He laughed and told me he would make sure people knew I was crazy, that I'd sound like a spurned woman and no one would believe me. No one was going to tell him whether or not he could talk to me."

"If he's alive," Sam said, "he won't be for long."

I squeezed his hand and continued. "I called the police, and they told me it was just a boyfriend dispute, and if I couldn't prove three instances where I feared for my life, there wasn't anything they could do. I was furious. I did everything I could to make my home safe, hired an expert to check my security. I hated that he'd made me afraid to go into my own house. Weeks passed and I was starting to relax.

"I had a cherished picture on my dresser. It was of me with my mom and dad right before she died. The frame and glass were broken and the picture of me had been cut into pieces. I filed an emergency restraining order against him. That absolutely flipped him out. Angie went nuts too. To this day I've never been able to figure out her reaction."

"Could she have been in love with him?" Jack asked.

"Wow, that's a concept I hadn't considered. She'd always been such a 'good wife,' but she's changed so much." I thought about it for a second, wondering if it could have been the reason she'd been so blind about him. "Very perceptive of you. That's possible. Certainly not at first, but over the years she always wanted to be with him. She loved talking to him because she felt Mark wouldn't listen to her."

"Continue," he said, no smile on his face or in his voice.

"After I filed the restraining order, it seemed to make me the object he needed to conquer. Angie seemed to encourage it. Jason lost his ever-lovin' mind. I always carry either a gun or a Taser when I show houses to people I don't know. Tragic things can happen when you walk into a house alone, not knowing who you might meet.

"Anyway, one night I came home and noticed immediately how dark it was. It seemed strange because I always left a light on. I figured a bulb had burned out, but it gave me an eerie feeling. When I flipped the switch, nothing happened. I was reaching into my purse for my Taser when the lights came on. There stood Jason. I was genuinely afraid."

"'You're not so stupid that you think I'll let you get away with this, are you?'" he asked.

"My first thought was that he was insane. The second was that I was in real danger."

Telling Jack and Sam this story, I could see it all again, and even though it had been months, it still had the power to rock me. "I had my hand around my Taser in my purse. I took a slow step backwards. Before I could blink, he struck me across the face - hard. I went to my knees."

I could feel the rage in Jack, could feel his whole body tensing.

"He kicked me. I was able to get the Taser turned on by the fourth strike. I got him in his leg. He went down. Then I got him in his shoulder. As fast as my broken rib would allow, I ran. He was still down when the police arrived. They arrested him. Angie came to see me twice to get me to drop the charges. I told her to never come back.

"I couldn't stay at my house any more. I stayed with Marge, my assistant. I stayed in Dad's cottage. I sold my house. When the trial was over, Jason only got seven months. I wanted out. Dad suggested I come here. He'd never let me come here before, so when I finally decided it would be okay to leave, I jumped at the chance. I haven't regretted it for a minute."

Jack was staring at me, but he didn't see me. His jaw was working. I looked at Sam and there was a lone tear falling down his roughened cheek. "Suppose Jack an' me woulda killed him if they hadn't locked his sorry ass up," he said, empathy turning to anger.

"I have so many things that keep going through my head. You spend a long time wondering if there was something you could have done to make it different. Did I lead him on in any way? How was it that Angie was so blind to what he was doing? For a while, I hated being alone. This place has gone a long way toward healing me."

Jack was gently rubbing his hand across my knee. It had become an absent habit, and I'm sure he wasn't conscious of it. There was nothing soothing about it. I got up and cleared the table that had been vacated and started helping Sam with the dishes.

Jack came up behind me, put his arms around my waist, and rested his chin on my head. In a quiet and sincere pledge, he said, "I'll kill Jason if he ever comes near you again – ever."

These men had become family in the short time I'd been here. It was a unique bonding. Leaving was going to be hard.

Chapter Seven

ELECTRIFYING

a gentle knock brought me awake the next morning. I grabbed my robe and opened the door without checking to see who it was.

"Don't ever do that again. Did you learn nothing from your experience?" Jack said harshly. "Even in this trusting town, it could have been anyone on the other side of that door."

"Why didn't you just use your key? It's never stopped you before," I sassed as I headed to the kitchen to set the coffee to brew. "Give me a minute. Let me splash water on my face and wake up. I'll be right out."

By the time I came out, the coffee was brewed and Jack was pouring two mugs.

"What brings you to my neck of the woods at this hour, sir?"

I was surprised to see it was already 6:30. "I must have been tired. I don't normally sleep this late."

"You're usually at the Amber Rose by now. I have to admit, I came up here to check to make sure you were all right."

"Why wouldn't I be?"

"I've thought of little else since our conversation yesterday. I can't get the image out of my head. I want to do damage to something, or preferably, someone. I want to take away the trauma it must have been so you don't ever have to think of it again. Bottom line - I feel frustrated there's nothing I can do to make it right."

We stood facing each other, speaking without using words. Sometime over the past few weeks I knew I wanted to pursue a relationship with him. I knew he occupied most of my waking and sleeping thoughts, and I was feeling bold enough to voice what I wanted.

"There's probably something you could do to erase the imagine for a few minutes," I said brazenly, holding his gaze.

"And what might that be?" He was barely breathing.

"You can kiss me the way you did a few weeks ago. That might help me forget." A devilish smile crossed my face as I wondered who had taken over my rational mind and put those words in my mouth.

"Did you honestly just say that then blush?" Jack asked quietly as he put his mug on the counter.

"I'm not sure where those words came from, but I'm sure they couldn't have been from *my* mouth."

"You definitely threw the gauntlet. I've been watching nothing but your lips, and I assure you, that's exactly where they came from." He took my face in his hands and proceeded to cover my lips with his.

Part of me was conscious that this was the most electrifying feeling my body had ever known. I wanted to repeat it, wanted to feel it again. Every pore was singing with excitement . . . no, not singing, screaming. If the world ended this minute, I'd die a happy woman.

"Not sure exactly what you're doing, but honest to God, no one's ever kissed me like that in my life. Please don't stop."

He pressed me against the counter so the full lengths of our bodies were touching. "It must be you, because I'm pretty sure I've never wanted to kiss someone the way I want to kiss you."

My hands threaded through his wavy hair as I brought him

closer. I wanted to absorb him. This was magic, and I was transported by the feelings sweeping through me.

My hands were restless, my body intense. I wanted to touch him, all of him. I wanted to feel his strength. I touched his face. I ran my hands down his arms that were around me, intoxicated with his strength, with the passion he ignited. He lifted me to the counter as I wrapped my legs around him and pulled him even closer. My silky robe slid from my shoulders, exposing my breasts to his wandering hands.

"Do you always answer the door like that?" he groaned against my neck.

"You woke me up from a sound sleep. I covered up," I said. "What more did you want?"

"You have no idea how much more I want. Is this the way you sleep?" he breathed, stepping back to look at me, to run his thumbs over my already hardened nipples.

"Every time I close my eyes I'll have this vision. Perfection, absolute perfection," he whispered as his lips took mine. We could have been there a minute, it could have been an hour. It didn't matter. The sensations swirling through me had me wanting more.

When his lips left mine to travel down my neck, I wanted only his intensity. I wanted to feel him, and feel what I was doing to him. When he took my nipple in his mouth and ran his tongue over it in the same way he'd danced with my tongue, I let out a deep moan.

He came back to my lips, consuming them, gentle then hard, tongues warring, then gentled again into a slow dance to a tune heard only by us. One by one, I undid the buttons of his shirt, never breaking contact with his lips, never wanting this feeling to stop. My hands circled his waist to release the shirt from the confines of his jeans, but he stilled them.

He pulled my robe from my shoulders, freeing me to explore. "Not yet, we have plenty of time."

And yet the kisses became more intense, more drugging, making me wet and throbbing as his hand found my desire and caressed me, making me sigh with pleasure. As his finger entered me, I was sure I was crossing into heaven. His thumb stroked me as our tongues continued to duel. He gentled me to the counter.

Lying there, vulnerable, exposed, his hands caressing me like a treasure, he whispered, "You're stunning. So much more than I even imagined."

His lips started at my navel, sending flames through my arousal. His thumbs were gentle on my mound, opening me to touch, to explore, to enjoy. When his mouth touched me, I cried out.

He covered me with his lips, stroked me with his tongue. I put my legs over his shoulders and opened up.

"Such a delicate rose bud," he said against me as his finger slid easily inside. Within minutes, his lips and his tongue moving in rhythm had me on the brink. "Ready?"

"No, I don't want it to be just about me."

"I told you, we have all the time in the world. Let go and enjoy."

When I came, I knew every cell in my body was involved. I was so satisfied and he was so tender. I'm not sure I could have moved on my own.

"Put your arms around my neck."

"While I appreciate the thought, I'm not so little."

Without missing a beat, he had my legs around his waist and pulled me against him, skin to skin. He was kissing me. I was almost delirious, tasting me on his lips. The kiss deepened, and we were in the bedroom before I was conscious we'd moved. I felt protected, cared for, safe. I'd been so lost in the magic of the kissing I was surprised to feel his tongue circling my nipple.

"Not so fast, mister. It's my turn."

His zipper was undone, and I made a ritual of removing his jeans. My warm tongue tasted him along his muscle ridges as his pants were finally removed.

"Magnificent," was the only word I could think of as I worked my way back to his manhood. Jack held my head as I took him into my mouth, guiding me, encouraging me.

I nibbled and sucked, tongued and caressed. I took him deep in my throat, then teased his tip. Over and over I took him in my cheek, against my lips, wrapped in my tongue, loving the taste and feel and texture of him. My hands roamed his biceps, his stomach, his shaft. I wanted him desperately.

It wasn't long before he was spent. He wrapped me in his arms, my head resting on his chest.

"I'm not sure how that just happened. I've thought of little else the past few weeks, but that wasn't at all my intention when I came over this morning."

He ran his fingers through my hair, stopping at the end to twirl a strand into a curl. It seemed he did it unconsciously, but it was a tender gesture.

"You'll never hear me say I'm sorry," I sassed as I hopped out of bed, surprisingly carefree in my lack of clothing.

"You're right about that. Not an experience that will ever be defined by the word 'sorry.'"

After retrieving and zipping his pants, he found my robe and put it around my shoulders as he pulled me into a soul-searing kiss. "Cover up or all of my good intentions will be gone in a flash."

"For what purpose do you have good intentions, sir? Sounds pretty boring to me." I pushed my arms into my sleeves and tied the sash.

"Busy day ahead, and you're a tempting distraction."

"Not at all how I thought to spend my morning, but I bet I'll be smiling all day," I said, putting my arms around his neck and drawing him in for another indescribable kiss. I whispered against his lips, "Come up and see me again sometime."

His eyes held mine. He ran his thumb across my cheek. "Don't tempt me." He swatted my butt playfully. "I need to get out of here or the whole day will be spent discovering your secrets."

"Promises, promises." His lips devoured me, then he was gone.

What a complex man, intriguing, intelligent, and wholly irresistible.

As the day progressed, I tried to work on an article for a publication that had a fast-approaching deadline. I found it hard to concentrate, and had no idea if it made any sense. I'd have to read it later to know what I'd said.

EDGY AND DISTRACTED, I HOPPED IN MY CAR AND STARTED DRIVING. The weather was cool but sunny. There were a lot of small towns nearby that I hadn't yet explored. Caribou was not too far up the road. The former silver mining town was now a ghost town, and I'd wanted to take pictures there for a while. The sun and warmth, combined with my tingling senses and diverted mental state, were a great combination for what I had in mind. I couldn't have been more pleased.

Caribou was exactly what I was looking for that day. There wasn't much there, only a few stone ruins and a dilapidated wooden building, but that kept me busy for hours. And then I wandered, roaming through the hills, driving the back roads, stopping frequently to take pictures of things that caught my eye.

Sometime during the late afternoon, I found myself in Boulder. I stopped at a familiar hangout to grab a bite to eat, all the while thinking of Jack, thinking of the morning, feeling like a teenager with a crush, smiling a secret smile when I remembered. By the time I got to Nederland, the sun was down but the lights were still on at the Amber Rose. I stopped to see Sam.

A matronly patron was leaving, and I stepped back to hold the door open for her. Sam's scowl turned to a bright smile when he saw me coming in.

"What has you looking like such a grump, my friend?"

"That was ol' Morning Sun. What a complete misnomer. She ain't nothing like her name."

"I take it she's not gonna be warming your bed anytime soon?"

Sam made a noise that sounded like a bark and snickered as he wiped down the counter. "Nicest thing I can say about ol' Morning Sun is that she ain't a twin."

When I realized what he'd said, we broke into laughter.

"No wonder they call you Wicked Sam. You're awful."

"I do my best," he said. "Getcha a cuppa coffee?"

"Not tonight, but thanks. I stopped in to see your old face. I wanted to tell you what a treasure you are."

Blushing, he leaned across the bar and patted my hand. "I always knew you, even though you didn't know me, so I feel like this is your home. But I gotta say, I been finding myself getting madder and madder about that story you told. Wish I could have five minutes with that varmint."

"I love that about you, your unconditional acceptance. But here's a big lesson I learned from Jason. I won't let anyone steal my joy anymore. He's not the one that gets to be in charge of my life. It was awful what happened, but let me help you let go of it like you've helped me."

"Can't help but think about what woulda happened to you. You change lives. I'm glad you're here."

"There's nowhere I'd rather be."

On the short drive home, I thought about how laid back this life was in comparison to what I'd known up until this point. Perspective is a strange thing. I was having a paradigm shift about what was important in my life and what wasn't.

Completely relaxed, all I wanted was to finish my day in the 'pond' they called a bathtub. The water fanned out from the shower head like a waterfall. As I slid under the warmth of the flowing water, I laughed at the random things that reminded me of Jack, like the ocean blue of the tub being the color of his eyes. I was smitten, no doubt about it.

So smitten that I thought I conjured him up when I opened my eyes and saw him staring at me in the mirror. I closed my eyes, slid deep into the water, and laughed out loud.

"What's so funny, little one?"

"*Jack?*" I said, splashing water as I came up hurriedly.

"You were expecting someone else, maybe?"

"I'd be lying if I said I minded you showing up at random hours." I blushed in response to my loose tongue and slid deeper under the water. He sat on the edge of the magnificent tub that was worked into the mountainside.

"Your most attractive quality, in my opinion, is that you don't seem to have a filter on your honesty. I'm often surprised you don't hide behind guile. I've thought of little else all day."

"You've 'thought of little else all day' meaning my honesty?" I asked.

Smiling, he looked at me, the vision I'd just been comparing to the blue of the pool. "Thought of little else all day besides you and many of your facets," he said, walking across the room to get a towel from the heated holder.

"My facets or my assets?"

"Yes," he said.

As he approached, he held the towel open to wrap me in. "Wondering how in the world you've come to occupy so much of my thought space. Wondering about the magnet you have that keeps drawing me back. Wondering what kind of spell you've cast that I can't seem to break."

Shocked at his words, at the significance behind them, at what they did to my entire being, I stepped into the towel, into his arms, and said quietly, "You don't want to, do you?"

I felt his body still. "Don't want to what?"

"Break the spell."

He relaxed against me. "Certainly not tonight. None of this was in my plans, but nothing could have kept me away. I've been hard for you all day, thought of the taste of you, the way you move under my lips, and have wanted you moving under me since the moment I walked out of here."

"Well isn't *that* a coincidence? I've been thinking of your lips all day, wondering if you inject them with drugs, imagining the magic they hold, and how they draw so much out of me. It appears as though we're sharing an addiction," I smiled as I headed to the bedroom and lit a solitary candle, "an addiction that could easily become an obsession."

When he pulled my bath-warmed body against him, I shivered. I could feel the length of his hardness. I moaned deeply.

"I can't remember ever wanting anything like this," he said against my lips. His mouth slid down my body, slowing at my breasts, my navel, then my warmth that was writhing in wait for him.

I clutched his hair, holding on because I never wanted this sensation to stop. "Please," I begged, "I want you. Don't stop."

He worked his way up my eager body, kissing my lips in a way that was becoming familiar and necessary to my sanity.

"Please," I said again.

"Please, what?"

"Please help me," I said breathlessly. "I need you . . . now."

He slid his hard tip against me. Slid his wet hardness gently over my most sensitive area as I moved, needing more of him. He continued to kiss me, drug me, embrace me. My hand reached for him, guiding him into my waiting moistness. Slowly, gently at first, his kisses activated every nerve in my body until I was desperate.

When I couldn't stand it any more, he entered me completely, solid, deep, wet, all the while working in a motion as ageless as time. But now it was our time, and I couldn't get enough.

As he filled me, brought me to the brink, slowed, then brought me to the brink again, he said softly against my lips, "Are you ready?"

"Jack . . ."

"Imagine we're on a ledge." His voice was tender as he moved harder inside me. "You and I are the only ones who'll ever know where this particular cliff is. We're the only ones who'll ever be able to revisit this memory we're creating . . . this interlude when our worlds stand still, if only for a moment."

His words entranced me. The spell he wove was magical. "I want to watch you melt for me, pulling me in." I'm not sure I actually cried out his name as I found fulfillment, but my whole being called to him.

When I started to unravel, he was there with me. I felt his release, felt him tighten inside me, felt his body shiver gently. Holding me in his arms, he rolled to his back. "You're exquisite. I've pictured you this way dozens of times, but never came close to the reality."

We spoke quietly for a while. "I think you've hypnotized me." He ran his fingers through my hair, twisting the end into a curl. He kissed me, then sat up abruptly.

"You're not leaving, are you?" I hoped I didn't sound desperate, but I couldn't bear for the night to end.

He turned back, resting on an elbow as he pulled the cover away from my body. "You are perfection," he said, almost matter-of-factly as his eyes covered me where his hands had been a short while ago. "No, I'm not leaving. I'm gonna lead you to your alluring shower and lather every inch of your body with soap and my hands."

"Then what are you waiting for?" How could his words inflame me again?

The shower would be a memory that lived with me forever. Tender, passionate, playful, serious, intense, I was finding a side of Jack I could get used to.

"Do you do this often?" he asked, almost hesitantly.

"You mean take showers with tall, dark, handsome men in a remote cabin in the middle of nowhere?"

"No, are you *with* many men?"

Sensing my answer was important, I took the bar of soap and started lathering his chest. "It's been years. I've been sidetracked, first with my mother's illness and death, then throwing myself into my work to prove something, although I'm not sure any more what I was trying to prove. Then there was the debacle with Jason.

"Until I walked into the Amber Rose and saw you standing there talking to Sam, there hasn't been one man in as long as I can remember who's made my heart flutter, ignited my senses, or made me *want* the way you do."

"My turn," he said, taking the soap. "Put your hands against the wall and lean forward," he said hoarsely, soaping my shoulders, cupping my breasts, running his slick hands down my spine.

When he came to the base of my spine, his hands stilled, then gently moved lower. I leaned further forward, pushing out to get more of his attention. I felt him rubbing against me. "It takes nothing for you to get me this way."

His hands came around to my front, sliding into my hidden folds, enticing with his soapy hands while he guided himself into me from behind. "That feels amazing." Was that *my* voice sounding so distant? But I didn't want words just then, only to feel.

I reached behind me and wrapped my fingers around his shaft. Soapy and slick, he grew even harder as I held him in my grasp, milking, pressing, coaxing. The warm water and woodland setting added to the enchantment of the moment as we reached a shattering climax together.

Spent, I turned in his arms and began what could easily become my favorite waking pastime, kissing Jack. By the time we'd dried each other, we collapsed into the softness of the king sized bed, cuddled in the middle.

"I'm glad tomorrow's Sunday," I said with my eyes closed. "Not sure I'll have the fortitude to meet anyone and be coherent for a while. Not sure I'll even be able to stand."

He kissed the top of my head and wrapped his arms around me even tighter. "Sleep as long as you can."

Chapter Eight

CLARK

When I woke sometime before the sun came up, Jack and I were spooning. I could feel the length of him and wondered at his amazing prowess. "It's only you," he whispered, reading my mind. "It's always there, just below the surface, the desire for you never goes away."

"Listening to you makes my heart beat faster," I blushed. "I love your words."

I rolled on top of him, my hair framing our faces. When we started kissing, I couldn't believe I could want him again. I started moving against his rigidity. I rubbed my breasts against his chest.

"I want to taste you again," he said softly, cupping my hips and drawing me forward. I inched forward so I was positioned over his face, my hands against the wall holding me steady. I rocked back forth over him, my thighs tightened as his hands drew me even closer. I leaned back and took him in my hand, stroking, exciting until I couldn't stand it anymore.

It was such pleasure to slide over him, slick, hot, ready to ride his strength. This morning our interlude was gentle, slow, so intimate and tender I wanted to weep. If I had designed the perfect lover, I couldn't have imagined anything more I could want. We took our time . . . serious, playful, soul-searing. We came together in a tangle of tongues and emotion. It was glorious.

We reached consciousness several hours later, sun high, bodies famished for food.

He pulled on his jeans, I pulled on his shirt with only one button holding it closed. Our camaraderie continued as we made a huge breakfast of freshly squeezed orange juice, bread, bacon, and eggs.

"No way I could eat like this normally," I laughed, "but I think I've worked off enough calories in the past twelve hours to make this an acceptable exception."

We shared funny childhood stories and poignant memories. He told me how he met my father not too long after Jack moved to town, and how they struck up a close and companionable relationship. Jack told me he helped my dad work through some decisions while building this hideaway, and they'd remained close over the years.

"What do you have on your agenda today?" he asked.

"I was gonna do some editing of the great shots I got yesterday at Caribou."

"I've been around long enough to know some places you might find interesting. I'm happy to be the tour guide if you want to grab your camera. When we're done, we'll get a bite of dinner. Only thing you might want is a change of shoes."

The thought of spending the day with Jack, carefree, alone, undivided attention . . . my heart raced at the prospect as I got my equipment together, putting on the appropriate clothing for rocky jaunts. Jack packed a small travel bag of water, snacks, and other items that might come in handy while we were out.

"Thanks for the loan of your shirt," I said saucily, tossing it back to him. "Much as I hate to cover up that gorgeous chest of yours, it's probably best."

"Not sure I'll ever see this shirt again without seeing you in it. It's a lot better looking on you. We have several options. Have you taken pictures at Sugarloaf yet? Gold Hill?"

"Not yet. I didn't know if there was anything to see in Sugarloaf, seeing as how it's only about two square miles."

"I know where to take you then. We'll make a few stops and I'll turn you on to some completely different experiences," he said as we loaded up the Cruiser.

"Your very existence turns me on. Lead on, Macduff."

He turned out of my driveway and headed to the heart of town. "Are you aware that's a misquote?"

"Oh, my God, you crack me up. Is there anything you're not aware of? *I'm* aware of it but would never have pegged you for a Shakespeare buff."

"I'm not, I just like the original meaning better. With you, 'Lay on, Macduff' could take on a whole new meaning."

The joy of the morning began our carefree, flawless day. The weather was warm with a few clouds for contrast, the leaves were full of color, the companionship blissful. Wherever we went, if there were people, they knew Jack.

"Is there anywhere we could go where the people don't know you?"

"You spend enough time wandering around up here where there aren't that many people, you're bound to run into the same ones sooner or later," he said with a smile.

"Before we head out of town, let's head over to the Carousel of Happiness," he offered. "In addition to being a work of art, it's unusual to have such a display in an out-of-the-way place like this."

I'd heard fascinating stories about it, and couldn't wait to get unique shots. The larger-than-life figures of the Carousel, all hand carved, were a distinctive blend of vintage and imaginatively new, with bursts of bright colors. The traditional calliope carousel music added to the flavor of the experience. I was in seventh heaven capturing not only the overall feeling, but also the unique blends of fanciful adaptations of Victorian and 21st Century entertainment.

"Each of the fifty-eight life-sized creatures was hand carved by an ex-Marine, and each one represented something special," Jack said. "He kept a vision in his mind of a carousel in a mountain meadow to help him survive the horrors of Viet Nam back in the 60s."

"This must've taken him forever."

"Well over two decades, but it was a town project, and all of the profits go to charity. He wanted to help kids with disabilities, especially those in small Colorado mountain communities, so it's fully handicap accessible. Scott Harrison is a great guy. This was the definition of a unifying project. Almost everyone in town had some part in it. It's so much more than just an attraction."

"The story is almost as captivating as the Carousel itself. It takes on an even greater appeal knowing its history." Jack helped me to see and feel new things at each place we stopped. I couldn't imagine any more capacity in my heart to hold the emotions he was creating.

We headed into Boulder for dinner. We stopped at an out-of-the-way Italian restaurant that appeared intimate but not too fancy, the sign proclaiming it to be *Bertolino's Trattorio*. The owner greeted Jack with a hug of genuine affection. "It's been way too long, my friend. It's so good to see you. Where have you been keeping yourself?"

"Staying in Nederland most of the time these days. Like the way of life better, like the people a whole lot better."

"It is truth, Jack, it is truth. And, che bella donna! Who is your magnificent lady?"

"This is Callie Weston. Callie, my old friend, Angelo Bertolino."

"Certainly my pleasure," I smiled as Angelo leaned over to kiss my hand.

"Weston? Are you the daughter of Charles?" he asked, surprised, looking at Jack.

A look passed between them that I didn't understand, but was confusing when Jack shook his head, "She is the daughter of Charles."

"Let me lead you to your table. It is good to see you again," he said, gesturing to a corner table that was secluded from other diners. "Gianna will be right with you. Will you both have wine?"

"Yes, please," we said in unison.

"What was that about?"

"What specifically are you asking?"

"How does he know my father?"

"Your father and I came here while Charles was building his *Fortress of Solitude*," Jack chuckled. "I always loved that name. It was so appropriate."

"And the other thing . . ."

Just then, Gianna showed up with our wine and menus. After pleasant hellos and introductions as Angelo's daughter, Gianna asked if we might like to share the evening special, a family recipe that had been passed down from her great-grandmother.

"How could we refuse?" I smiled sweetly as the charming young woman who was heavy with child left to place our order.

Angelo brought bread straight from the oven. He grated cheese and ground pepper onto a dipping plate, then explained how they made their own oils. "You will find none to compare, Bella," he said with an exaggerated bow.

"You need to watch him," Jack said, sotto voce. "He is the consummate ladies' man."

Angelo looked from one to the other and said, "You have chosen well, my friend."

Without addressing Angelo's remark, Jack said, "And it looks like congratulations are in order, old man. When are Gianna and Teo expecting?"

"She has three more months. Teo believes he has invented fatherhood, and sometimes I shoo him away because he hovers like an old hen over a young chick. She would get nothing done if I didn't send him on regular errands." The men laughed as Gianna arrived with our meal.

"Enjoy yourselves. We will leave you in peace. If you have need of anything, you know you have only to ask."

There was a scoop of polenta on each end of the oval plate, with a delectable looking dish in the middle.

"This food is almost orgasmic," I said after taking my first bite, a slight moan in my voice. "How long have you known Alberto?"

"I discovered him while doing graduate work in Boulder, so it's been at least a decade."

The door opened and a couple came in laughing. "What did you major in?" I asked, taking another delicious bite.

When he didn't answer, I looked up and saw Jack frozen in place. I heard Angelo say in a friendly manner, "What a coincidence, Clark, that Jack is here also."

Clark was an attractive man who appeared to be about Jack's age. He was with a picturesque woman with long, dark hair whose eyes lit like a hungry cat when she saw Jack. "Well, well, who's your friend, lover, and why haven't I met him before?" She almost purred.

I was watching Jack, motionless, no expression, staring at the man standing a few feet away. "Aren't you going to introduce us, Clark?" his willowy date said seductively.

"No, he's not," said the sudden stranger sitting rigid and cold next to me, his eyes never leaving Clark. "He's gonna remember he has an engagement elsewhere and leave while he can still walk."

All eyes had been on Jack during his surprising outbreak, but they were now focused on Clark.

"He's absolutely right, Ali, I just remembered we have reservations elsewhere," said the man who was leading her out the door. "Sorry for any trouble, old man," he said, hitting Angelo on the shoulder. "Maybe some other time."

I tried to make things normal. I tried to overlook what had happened, but Jack ignored me. I tried to interact with Angelo or Gianna, but the entire evening had been ruined.

"Would you like a cannoli to finish your meal?" asked Gianna quietly.

"No, just the check," Jack said, no smile, no light in his eyes, almost frightening.

He stood, dropped a small pile of bills on the table, and held the door open for me. I told Angelo and Gianna goodbye, but it was subdued.

When we were in the car heading home, I very quietly asked, "May I ask who that was?"

"No."

We traveled the dark canyon in silence. I felt cheated that my dream day had become a nightmare. This man bore no resemblance to the friend I had come to cherish over the past few weeks. The minutes grew longer, the dark pressed in, and I wanted to scream, to get at least some small explanation of what had happened.

When we pulled into the driveway, Jack got out, opened my door, opened the back door and got out my equipment. He unlocked the house, put my things on the counter, and turned without looking at me. He said, "I'll see you soon, Callie."

I stood in front of him. "Jack, listen to me," I pleaded. "I'm not the enemy, I'm your friend. Won't you please talk to me? If we can't communicate, we don't have much foundation."

He finally looked down at me, as though focusing for the first time in over an hour, as though coming back to some kind of reality. "No, you're not the enemy," he said as he kissed me on the forehead and walked away.

I WAS LOST. THINGS HAD BEEN SO GOOD, AND EARLIER TODAY WAS something I never could have imagined, even hoped for. How could he do this? Who was Clark and what happened between them that could have caused such a violent reaction in my otherwise levelheaded Jack?

My night was restless. I kept reliving the morning, the afternoon, seeing the flawlessness of it. And then I would remember the evening, and the perfection shattered at my feet. The circles under my eyes were dark the next morning, but I didn't care. I wanted to see Jack, wanted to understand. I needed the familiar around me.

The roller coaster of yesterday had me feeling off balance. It was starting to snow, but I bundled up and headed to see Sam. At the sound of the bell, Sam looked up. Seeing my face, he lost his smile and opened his arms. I was in them immediately.

"What's going on, pun'kin? Tell ol' Sam what has you so sad."

"He left, just up and left."

"He gets it in him every now and again. I'm darned sure he don't know what to do with you. You fry all his circuits. He knows what he knows, and you don't look anything like what he knows is truth. Just you wait. He'll come around soon."

"It wasn't me who made him run." I sat at the counter and laid my head on my arm. "I wondered if you might know where he was."

What a tender soul my Sam was. He patted my hair and said briskly, "If I knew the answer, I'd track him down myself and whip the daylights outta him for doing this to you."

I raised my head and we both laughed at the image that created. "I'll pay admission to see it when it happens."

"You want some coffee?"

"Half a cup. Thanks for making me laugh." I wanted to tell him what had happened without telling too much. "Do you know his friend, Clark?"

"Ain't seen or heard of Clark in a long while. He was Jack's best friend. What's he done?"

Jack's best friend? How do people go from being best friends to the combative strangers I saw last night? Then I remembered Angie, and knew that sometimes life happens, and people don't always stay the same.

"He and Jack seem to have had a falling out," I said, noncommittally. "Jack seemed pretty upset when we ran into Clark yesterday. There was certainly no love lost between them."

Sam was as puzzled as I. "He sure got his share of demons."

My father said the same thing. What was I missing? What was chasing Jack? I was confused.

"Can I ask you something?"

"You know you can."

"Am I being foolish to pursue this with Jack? I mean, are his demons so big that he can't get past them?"

"I told you before, they don't come no better than Jack Franklin, and a good woman can love enough to heal old wounds. He weren't looking, so I imagine finding you kinda set him on his ear."

I thought about what Sam said, thought about what Jack and I had established the past few months, and was willing to take the risk to try to push through whatever it was that was haunting him - if he ever came back.

"Thanks, Sam, that helps. I'm gonna head back while the gettin's good. Will you close up and head on home? It looks like a blizzard out there."

"I'll be right behind you. Skedaddle now."

But I wasn't about to leave him to take care of the last-minute details, especially with how heavily the snow was falling. It took less than fifteen minutes with us working together to get everything shut down and locked up. All of a sudden, there was a deafening crack that shook the building to its core.

"What in the world was that?"

"That's what they call thundersnow. The clouds be pouring out the white, then *boom*, you get either the crack or the rolling thunder . . . thundersnow."

Sam insisted on driving me home. If I'd already been there, this would've been delightful, the fat snowflakes falling furiously. We hopped in his battered Jeep and took to the white covered roads like it was the middle of summer. "I'll wait 'til you get in." Sam dropped me close to the door. "Don't leave for nothing 'til this stops. This one's gonna be a doozie."

"Sure, sure."

I was thankful I hadn't tried to make the walk because just getting to the front door was a chore. I waved but wasn't sure he could see me, so I flipped the light a few times and he rumbled out of the drive.

Coming in the house hurt my heart. Everything about my

hideout reminded me of Jack. There weren't many parts of it he didn't occupy. I opened my computer hoping there'd be a message. Of course none of the emails were from him, but where had he gone?

The next morning turned to evening, and the snow was well over a foot deep with drifts much deeper. Had it only been two days ago we'd shared a lifetime, that we'd been as close as two people can be? My world was rocked that day not once, but twice, in completely different ways. Where was he? His phone kept going to voicemail. *"This is Jack. Leave a message."* I never did. He had to know I was calling.

Chapter Nine

I MISS YOU

*E*diting photos consumed my time. Every one brought back sweet memories. I had taken random shots of Jack throughout the day, and the wonder of what we had shared returned.

When I woke the next morning after a fitful night, the snow had stopped, but no one was going to be getting out for a while. I appreciated the scenery around me, but my heart hurt.

An afternoon and night of snow gave way to a shining landscape lit by a crisp, clear sky. It was breathtaking. Everything appeared to have been dusted with diamonds in the night. I wasn't foolish enough to venture out, but I opened two panels of glass doors that led from the kitchen, grabbed the shovel from the coat closet, and set about making a trail on the deck. The air was perfectly still and stunning.

Pulling on a sweater and retrieving the camera from my office, I wanted a diversion. For a few minutes it worked, but everywhere I looked I saw Jack. Even the blinding beauty of my surroundings couldn't bring solace for long. He had to have been hurting to leave like this, didn't he? I wanted to be sympathetic, but I was getting angry. Had I been so off base to trust him? It wasn't just what we'd shared this week. We'd spent months becoming friends, sharing our lives, establishing what I believed was a foundation. Both Sam and my father thought he was the best, but would the best react this way, completely forgetting my existence?

I needed something to do to occupy my mind. I wrote letters to clients I hadn't contacted in a while, edited more photos, cleaned an already spotless kitchen, prepped food for the coming week. I called Sam to make sure he was okay. I went hours without thinking of Jack – but the only consecutive ones were when I was asleep.

I had a sadness for him at whatever had caused this reaction, and a huge ranking because he was doing this. I sat down to write him an email.

Dear Jack
I miss your words
I miss your lips
I miss the words from your lips
that make my body burn
I miss your lips on mine
I miss your lips on me
I miss standing in your arms
I miss the passion
your words can excite
I miss your voice
The loudest thing in my head
I miss the way you touch me
with just words
But more than anything else
I miss my friend
Whom I thought I could trust
My heart aches for you
I miss you
I miss us . . . passionately

But I didn't send it. After working a while, I closed my computer and sat. Was his distrust so great this was the only way he could deal with it? Obviously Clark was a big part of what was going on, but was there a woman behind their animosity? How could I not take some of this personally? I was too alone with my thoughts.

EXHAUSTED WHEN I WOKE, I COULDN'T WAIT TO HOP IN THE SHOWER and get my body going. I had to meet clients in Denver in a few hours.

On my way out of town, looking more refreshed than I felt, I headed to Sam's for my morning cup. The coffee and the drive revived me. I needed to focus on the day ahead. I'd spoken with the Dunlap's on many occasions, and knew the homes I'd selected were exactly what they were looking for. All were near where they'd be working, and all fit exactly their expressed needs. I'd made videos for them when I previewed homes, and we narrowed it down to three. They were excited to find their new place, and I couldn't let what was going on in my life affect their special time.

Before I got into Denver, my phone rang. "Sometimes I can be a real jerk," Jack said quietly.

"As long as you recognize that truth, I won't have to point it out."

"Can you forgive me for leaving like that?"

"Where are you?" I took deep breaths, not wanting my heart rate to affect my voice.

"I'm heading back to town. I'd like to come by, but won't blame you if you don't want to see me."

"I'm headed to Denver. I have a full day ahead of me. Let me call when I get back, see how we're both feeling then." I wasn't sure how I felt. I'd missed him so much, but I was truly hurt.

"I'm sorry, Callie."

The enjoyment of seeing my assistant Marge after almost a month, and the arrival of the Dunlaps shortly thereafter took my mind off Jack. The Cherry Creek area of Denver was expensive and well kept. A few brightly colored leaves still clung to the trees in their previous autumn glory in spite of the recent snow. The colors, crisp air, and bright sun made the time seem idyllic for house hunting.

They liked the first two houses, but I'd saved the best for last. The elderly lady who owned it was no longer able to live alone, and her children had moved her to a nursing home. They were selling at a greatly reduced price to get it sold in a hurry. I knew how much they had liked the others, but this, I was confident, would be a perfect fit. I was excited to show them.

A man ran out the front door as we pulled in the driveway. Feeling uneasy and knowing something wasn't right, I took note of his license number as he hopped in his car and sped off. I advised the Dunlaps to stay in the car until I'd checked on the situation.

Mr. Dunlap would have none of it and accompanied me to the front door that was standing open. There was a large amount of what appeared to be blood on the entryway walls and floor. I pulled my gun from my thigh holster and saw the shock register on Mr. Dunlap's face.

"Here are my keys. Go back to the car and call 911. Have them send an ambulance."

"I'm not gonna leave you to go in there alone."

"I appreciate that, but I'm well trained," I said in a whisper, "and we need the police."

"Then wait for them."

"It may be too late by then."

After hesitating only a moment, he ran to the car.

I knew I should wait, but what if the person who was bleeding was still alive? I needed to act quickly. I removed my heels and tiptoed into the main room. I'd been here before and knew the layout of the house. I listened intently but heard no sounds.

When I was confident no one was on the first floor, I followed the trail of blood up the stairs, gun drawn, nerves controlled, hoping beyond hope I was not too late. The trail of blood led to the closet in the master bedroom at the top of the stairs. I made sure my back was protected, then called out. No one answered. I crept quietly toward the door and opened it. What I found left my stomach heaving.

An older woman was lying on the floor, cowering, her hands covering her head. Clothes torn, blood everywhere, she whispered, "Don't hurt me."

"It's okay, it's okay. I'm going to help you. Don't be afraid. Who did this?" I said, panic from my own ordeal screaming through my mind.

"There was a man," she said faintly. "Must've heard you . . . ran away." She started to cry. I comforted her, visions of Jason clouding my brain. I wanted to scream, but understanding her nightmare gave me resolve to share my hard-won strength.

"Where are you hurt?" I asked quietly.

"All over." She was growing weaker. "I'm Christie Baynard . . . an agent." She took deep breaths. "Office called. Said someone wanted . . . to see . . . didn't think . . . swung by . . ."

She started to cry again, recounting her horror.

"Don't talk," I said, "the ambulance should be here soon."

The sirens could be heard in the distance. "Don't leave me," she said. "Please don't leave me. What if he comes back? Please stay with me."

"My name's Callie, Callie Weston. It's okay, Christie, it's okay. I'm not going anywhere. You're safe now."

"I know you," she said faintly. "Please stay."

I took her hand and spoke gently, remembering the fear, remembering the pain, gently getting her hair out of the blood on her face.

"Are you married, Christie?"

"No . . . husband died . . . five years . . . three kids . . . in college."

"Don't talk anymore. You're gonna be fine."

"We're up here," I called when I heard the commotion downstairs. "Top of the stairs, first room."

Guns drawn, the police came in with barrels pointing straight at me.

"It's okay," I said, laying my weapon on the blood-soaked carpet, raising my hands so they were visible. "She's been hurt, she needs an ambulance."

Medics were coming in with a stretcher, so I stood to give them access.

"Don't leave me, Callie," Christie said fearfully.

"I'm right here. You're safe. I'll stay with you."

"Can you tell us what happened, ma'am?" the older officer asked.

"My name's Callie Weston. I'm a Realtor. I brought clients to see the house. When we pulled into the driveway, a man ran out, jumped in his car and sped off. I got his information."

"Good work," he said as I gave him make, model, and license number.

"Her name is Christie Baynard. She came to show the property and no one was here yet, so she unlocked the front door and walked through the house, turning on all the lights. She was expecting a husband and wife to show up." I told them the story, just as she had told me.

"When she came down the stairs, the prospective Buyer was coming through the front door. She extended her hand to introduce herself, the man turned, locked the door, and pulled a knife. She didn't remember much after that, only that he cut her and she ran up the stairs. When he found her, he hit her and cut her several more times."

My mind flew back to the time I'd walked in and found Jason. I remembered the moment it registered my life was in danger, and I was confronting a crazy man. I thought about how terrifying it must have been for her, alone in the house, door locked. I knew well the shock of the unexpected, and how it would have taken her a moment to realize what was happening.

She was in a vacant house with a mad man. How many times do we show houses in similar situations with no forethought of who we're meeting? Thoughts of my own night were clawing at me, pulling me to break down as I relived the memory of my horror.

My mind was racing – after this I will change my showing habits, I'll integrate this into my classes for men as well as women, more safety rules will be put in place. And then I remembered the one reality that always snapped me out of my journey into darkness - I would not allow Jason to continue to terrorize me. I'd won. He wasn't going to hurt me ever again.

"And?" the officer prompted me to finish my story.

"Oh, sorry," I said, trying to figure out where I'd left off. "The assailant must've heard us drive up. She said he stopped suddenly and ran. She crawled into the closet to hide, knowing he could follow her blood trail. The next thing she remembered, I was opening the door."

After giving them all the information I had, I promised to keep myself available, took the Dunlaps back to their car with a promise of contact the next day, and headed to the hospital to sit with Christie. When I called Jack it went to voicemail. I called Sam.

"Something's come up, Sam. I have to stay in Denver for a while. Have you seen Jack?"

"Nah, honey, he's still in the wind."

I told him briefly what happened. "You need me to come get you?"

"I appreciate it, but I'll be fine. I'm not sure when I'll be able to get out of here. When you see him, would you tell him I'll be back late tonight if I'm able?"

"I'll make sure he knows."

"Thank you. Oh, and Sam?"

"Yes, pun'kin?"

"I love you," I whispered as I hung up.

THERE WAS SO MUCH TO TAKE CARE OF - MORE POLICE INTERVIEWS, reports, just sitting at the hospital being available. As gruesome as her injuries were, thankfully they weren't life threatening. Her family was here, and they couldn't express enough how grateful they were we'd shown up when we did, and especially that I'd gotten a license number. The police were confident they would apprehend the suspect.

It was late that night when I headed home. It had warmed, but the skies were cloudy and drizzling. Running in from the rain, I shook my umbrella and collapsed it before turning into the room. He was leaning against my desk - as comfortable as though he'd never been gone.

I was thrilled – the heart quivers weren't from the run, they were from the sight of him. I stared, drinking in his lithe form, drunk from the excitement that he was there. Wanting to hold him but not knowing how to react. We were motionless, each absorbing the other. He held his arms open and I ran into them, hanging on for all I was worth. At that moment I didn't care where he'd been, I wanted him where he was right now.

"I'm so glad you're all right," he said, enfolding me in his strong embrace, running his fingers through my hair. "Sam told me. I was heading to Denver to be with you, but he said you were coming home. I didn't want to risk missing you, so I came here."

"Thank you," I said into his chest.

"I can't imagine what it's been like, but it sounds like you held your own."

Tears mingled with rain. Relief poured through me.

"Where have you been, Jack?" I hadn't meant to say the words, but I wanted to know.

"I needed some time. I know I handled things poorly, very poorly. I'm sorry. Clark and I go way back. He brought back a life I thought was long forgotten, but it was a selfish way for me to react."

I unwrapped myself from his arms. I tried to understand, tried to make sense of it. "What did you need time for?"

"Just time," he said, stepping forward and touching my hair, drinking me in as though he'd never seen me. "I'm glad you're safe."

The pain of the past few days flooded me. My heartache was tangible, crushing.

"There weren't phones where you were? No internet that you could have told me you were okay? No note to tell me you were alive? No *nothing*?" I raised my voice.

"I'm so sorry."

"Sorry? You're *sorry*?" I knew I sounded like a shrew. Knew it and wanted to do nothing to stop it. The relief I felt moments before became a consuming anger. "This has been because you needed *time*? Time from what, from us? From a past hurt you aren't willing to let go of?"

Suddenly I was drained. The stress of today, coupled with past few days, was more than I wanted to face right then. I walked to the door and picked up my umbrella.

"I couldn't explain because even I didn't understand," he said. "I was angry and hurt and felt like a wounded animal."

"So you thought it was okay to make me feel that way? You didn't see a need to even make contact? Didn't think our friendship even warranted the decency of a text?"

Without a backward glance, I stepped into the rain, the blessed, drenching rain. I started walking, oblivious to the elements, numb to everything.

Chapter Ten

SAM'S AWARD

*H*e was still there when I returned. Soaked to the bone, I knew I'd been foolish to be out in the drizzle. He had a fire blazing. He put his arm around me and led me to the bathroom. He removed my clothes and hurriedly removed his own. He guided me to the steaming shower and rubbed the feeling back into my limbs. My mind was lethargic.

After drying me, he carried me to the big bed, enfolding me in his arms under the covers. Touching, rubbing, warming. Softly he said, "I needed time to think. When I finished feeling sorry for myself, I realized what I'd done to you. I got back as quickly as I could. I'm truly sorry. I can't explain it, but it was never my intention to hurt you." I began to cry. "Please don't, little one. I can't bear that I've done this."

I said nothing, just cried as though I hadn't cried buckets the past few days. When there were no more tears, no more strength, I slept. I woke to the smell of bacon. I thought how wonderful it was to have someone like Jack to share my life, and then I remembered. I put on his shirt and stepped silently into the kitchen. His hair was tousled and he was standing at the stove in only his jeans.

Our eyes met. He turned off the stove and took me in his arms.

"That very sight has been with me day and night. I can't promise I won't ever hurt you again, but I'm truly sorry."

"Can you tell me about it?"

"I haven't dealt with it myself. For days I've only been reacting, not even facing it. Please believe I never meant to hurt you. I wasn't expecting Callie Weston to come crashing into my life. I didn't think I'd ever have to deal with someone like you. And you're even more frail than when I left."

I put my head against his chest, not knowing how to respond. Jack was here, he wanted me, he had demons. Could I help him? Could we get past them? I didn't know.

"Can you share some of it? Give me a clue what we're dealing with? You have to know it affects me as well, affects us."

"I'm not like you. My filter is much thicker than yours. I've never known honesty like yours. I know I shouldn't be surprised by it, but I always am. Promise me you won't ever stop."

"I'm not sure we can have what we want if I'm always waiting for the other shoe to drop, Jack. We'll never be able to sustain a relationship if I'm always worried you'll leave again."

"Will you trust me for a while? There are so many intersecting parts. Give me some time to figure it out, then I'll tell you as much as I can."

"Can you at least tell me what you want for *us*, or do you even want an 'us'?"

"I want *you*. I want what we've had for months. I want to share it all with you. I want your heart and your brains and your body and your friendship and your laughter and the way you think and the way you make me feel . . . I want it all."

The hurt and rejection were raw. I knew what *I* wanted was standing in front of me. We'd shared such joy, and I'd been so empty without him.

Pacing, I looked back at him. "I need to think. And I have to call the hospital and check on Christie."

Sitting on the edge of the bed, I called and spoke to her nurse. Christie was doing well, and they hoped she'd be able to go home in a few days. I sat for a few minutes after I hung up, considering how I wanted to proceed. I thought about Christie and Jason and how quickly life could change, that it could be over in the blink of an eye. Was what Jack and I had worth proceeding? I honestly thought it was. I was willing try to rid him of his ghosts.

I came out of the room and leaned against the kitchen counter. We held each other's gaze until I finally broke the silence. "You've never had the famous Callie Weston Pumpkin Pecan Pancakes with apple cider syrup. Sit down, cowboy, you're in for a treat."

He took my hand and pulled me to him. "Thank you. You're an extraordinary woman."

While I fixed his meal, I recounted Christie's attack and how it brought back so many unsavory memories. I told him how frightened she'd been, and what a blessing it was we showed up when we did. I shuddered to think what an entirely different outcome it would've been if we'd been five minutes later.

He kept touching me, hugging me, telling me how glad he was that Christie was okay, and how much it upset him that the scenario could just as easily been me. He cleaned the pan from the bacon, washed the countertops, made fresh coffee, then sat and listened.

I had finished the story of Christie's harrowing experience. We were reestablishing our foundation. "Where'd you go to school?" he asked as I folded pecans into the batter.

"Boulder. Got my degree in business with a minor in Psychology, then did the Real Estate Certification, then my MBA in Real Estate. Found that there's so much psychology involved in selling real estate that a four-year degree was a God-send many times over."

"I can only imagine. One of the reasons I live up here is because so many people you come in contact with are nuts, as you well know. I much prefer my own company, and obviously that of social misfits, rather than the lunatics who wander the streets in the guise of sane people."

"If you don't mind me asking, how do you afford to live up here?"

After a short pause, he got a twinkle in his eye and said, "You could say I'm a Jack of all Trades."

We laughed. "My father was a builder, too," he said. "I grew up pounding nails from as early as I can remember. I got into building when things were hot, made some good investments that paid off, and I'm comfortable enough to have as much free time as I want."

"The day you found me covered in mud, you were dressed in a suit."

"Good memory. I sit on a Board of Builders for the Denver/Boulder/Longmont area. Sometimes I have to look nice. Sometimes I have to play nice."

"*That* must be difficult," I said as I set his pancakes in front of him.

He was taking his first bite when I asked, "How often do you -"

"*Shhhhh*. Don't say a word." His eyes were closed. "These pancakes - they have to be experienced, savored, worshiped."

After a moment of silence he opened one eye and looked at me. "With the exception of you, I'm not sure I've ever had anything this delicious in my mouth."

I was inordinately pleased at his sensual reaction to being fed. "So have you heard the town is giving Sam the 'Coolest Small Business Owner' Award? They announced it yesterday."

A genuine smile crossed Jack's face. "No one in town deserves it as much as he does. He must be one happy guy."

"To say the least. His acceptance speech is next weekend and he's been having me help. It won't be anything but a drunken salute at the Pioneer Inn, but he's treating it like he's won a Nobel Prize. It's endearing."

"I'll head down and congratulate him, give him some speech ideas."

I groaned. "Don't you dare. The congratulations are fine, the ideas will get us all in trouble."

"Do you mind if I come back?" he asked softly from the doorway.

"What do you mean?"

He turned back to look at me, his hand on the doorknob. "I've been an ass. I've violated all kinds of trust issues. I'll do whatever I can to rebuild the bridges I tore down, but I don't want to presume. I don't ever want to take my welcome for granted."

"The past few days have been long. Just thinking of you being all the way down at the Amber Rose sets off a spark of panic." I smiled. "But thank you for asking. Yes, I'd appreciate it if you'd come back. I believe I like having you around."

HEADING HOME FROM BOULDER A FEW DAYS LATER, I GLANCED AT MY watch thinking it must be later than I thought. Sam rarely closed early and I was surprised to see it was only 6:30 and all of the lights were out. Going the few blocks out of my way to drive past his house, not only was his car there, but also the car that had been in front of the Amber Rose when I'd heard someone leaving through the back door. It was Morning Sun's car, parked next to Sam's. Was something wrong? Or maybe it was a social visit? Had I missed something right under my nose?

When I got home, I was glad to see Jack was there. He kissed me firmly on the lips as I came into the kitchen and set down my coat. "Is it possible that something's going on between Sam and Morning Sun?"

"Why would you think an off-the-wall notion like that?"

"Because the Rose was closed and Morning Sun's car is in his driveway, that's why."

"Can't imagine a less likely affiliation, but who knows? He'll tell us in his own good time if anything comes of it."

"How can you blow it off like that, Jack? Don't you want to know?"

"What should I say instead, my angel? That I know all about

it? That they've been seeing each other for a while? Fact of the matter is, I have no clue, and that's not a subject I care to speculate about. Now go wash up before your meal gets cold."

"Okay. I think it's really sweet to think of Sam having a lady friend. But she'll have to deal with me if she hurts him."

"You don't even know if they're seeing each other. Can we deal with facts?"

"Oh, sure . . . you go right ahead and burst my bubble." I was feeling sassy.

"Burst your bubble? Are you kidding? Have you *seen* Morning Sun?"

"Why, Jack Franklin, what a nasty thing to say. It doesn't matter what she looks like."

"It does to me. I sure couldn't sleep with her."

"Are you saying you wouldn't sleep with me if I wasn't cute?"

"You've got better things to put in my mouth than words. Now go, or I'll flip you with the edge of the dishcloth."

"That wouldn't be so bad."

With a raised eyebrow, he said, "It wouldn't?"

"Of course not. Then you'd have to kiss it to make it better."

Coming back in the room, I put my arms around his waist. "Thank you for the wonderful care you take of me. Today was long and exhausting, and there's no way I would've been able to fix myself something to eat if you hadn't done it for me."

"It's my pleasure to serve you, Ms. Weston. When you're done here, you can take a long soak while I clean up, then I'll give you a rubdown to help you sleep."

"Are you real?" I asked, stepping back to look into his enticing face.

"What do you mean?"

"Do people like you exist in the real world or are you a figment of my imagination? Am I going to wake up one day and find you're a phantom? Did I want you so badly I conjured you up?" With a sweet chuckle, Jack shooed me out of the kitchen.

True to his word, the rubdown put me immediately to sleep.

Sometime in the night I woke in his arms, having no memory of anything but warm oil seeping into my back with his expert touch. I wasn't sure what I'd done to deserve him, but I'd do everything in my power to keep him.

We were standing in the kitchen cleaning the remnants of breakfast. I loved this time of day, the peace and tranquility of our mornings together, the camaraderie.

"Okay, it's time. I have to go help Sam get ready. He's been telling me what he's going to say, and I keep telling him he only has five minutes, not fifty."

"I'll meet you over there," Jack said. "I have work I need to catch up on. Seems I waste all my waking hours figuring out your delights."

"Waste? You think of it as a waste?" I teased.

"Yeah, we can deal with the semantics of it later," he said, the affectionate smile I'd grown to love unfolding across his face. "In the meantime, try to help him find the limits of what to say. He can talk your ear off given the opportunity."

"I'll do what I can, but don't count on it. Besides, he's going be the star of the show. I'll just clip his wings a little."

POOR SAM WAS DRONING ON AND ON, AND EVERYONE IN THE ROOM was starting to get restless. I appreciated his generosity to the town, but he needed to be done. My feet were aching from standing most of the day, and the wall wouldn't hold me much longer. I thought it was cute that Morning Sun was sitting in the front row, hanging on every word. Maybe there *was* something going on. That old reprobate. I'd ask him when the time was right.

My heart started racing even before Jack nuzzled my neck. I could hear the smile in his voice when he whispered, "I have a bone to pick with you."

"Promises, promises, big fella. You take my breath away. Hot and moist with just a word. How do you do that?"

"I can still taste what I do to you."

"Okay, so you can pick your bone with me tonight, but make sure it's hard. God, I want you."

"Hard as a railroad spike – just the thought of you does that."

"Wish you could feel what your words have done." My voice was as low as I could make it.

"Think about me being tight in you. Standing here with no one the wiser, hard, hot, slippery."

"I'd climb on top."

"I love when you're on top," he whispered. "It means you move the way you want, and that ignites me."

"Then imagine me going up and down, sliding back and forth, squeezing." I tried to keep my voice low so none of the towns-people would hear. With an impish grin, I asked, "Do you think people would be shocked if they knew what we're talking about?"

"Nah, they know I can't keep my hands off you. All of me wants to please all of you. You have me so ready."

Candice was standing across the room. She winked and gave me a thumbs up. If it had been a secret before, it sure wouldn't be now.

"What happened last night was one of the most fantastic things my body's ever felt," I whispered. "I didn't know a woman could do that. I didn't know the body could feel such pleasure and not die from the sheer delight of it."

"Yeah, I have to admit my heart races at the thought of it. Makes me want to taste you all over again."

I tried to keep from moaning. "Doesn't matter what time of day it is, I want you. Sometimes I can't catch my breath for the want of you. I want my mouth on you right now."

"Don't push me. We may shock these good town folk after all if you keep it up."

"What matters is that *you* keep it up," I said.

"Wanna see? You cause this problem often. You're gonna need to take care of it soon."

"I love it when you threaten me like that . . ."

He got even closer. "I want to describe what you do to me. Always there, always aware. Can you taste me? Can you imagine your lips around me? I want you. I can feel you now, so swollen for you."

"You can touch my entire being with a memory, a word."

"We're gonna need to walk the walk soon. I'm pretty uncomfortable. Feel like a cord o' hard wood."

"I'll stay in front of you," I giggled. "Let's go."

Wishful thinking. Of course they wouldn't let their precious Jack Franklin just walk out. I'd been so busy using words to make love with Jack I hadn't heard the end of Sam's speech, but still it took fifteen minutes for us to get out of the building.

As Jack walked me to my car, he slowed. There were people filing out, but he didn't care. He took my face in his hands. "Your eyes look like emeralds in the lights' reflection."

He put his arm around my waist and turned me away from onlookers. "You're always with me. There's not much about you I don't love," he whispered against my lips.

My heart stopped, then thundered. He'd never actually told me he loved me, but I had no doubt. How could we have what we have and he not love me? It would just take time for him to say the words. He pulled me close. "Most of the time it's not overwhelming, it's just there. You're always gentle on my heart."

Magical words. I reached up to pull his face toward me so our lips could meet and saw we had an audience. Looking around, we grinned as the parking lot erupted into applause and catcalls and good-natured fun.

"You gonna make an honest woman outta her, Jack?" inquired one well-meaning neighbor.

"She's too pretty to let her get away," offered another.

Everyone was laughing as they walked by, slapping Jack on the back. He took my hand and walked me to my car. "Can we go to your place now?" he leered.

"That would be nice. I think we can find something to do."

Chapter Eleven

BOBCAT IN THE SNOW

e were standing at the expansive window in the living room, looking at the snow falling sideways over Barker Reservoir because of the wind. It was awesome. Much of the water was frozen, but the part that was thawed was mesmerizing, almost angry whitecaps. Jack's arms were around my waist and my head was leaning on his shoulder when suddenly I pulled free and ran to the closet. I wanted to get my winter gear so I could capture the power of the storm coming in.

"And where do you think *you're* going?" he asked as he leaned against the doorjamb of my bedroom.

"Stay or come with me. I'm gonna preserve some of the magnificence that's out there," I said excitedly.

"I know better than to argue, but you're not going alone. I'll get my coat." Within minutes we were bundled to face the elements and headed off for what Jack insisted would be no more than a fifteen minute outing.

"Quarter of an hour, no more," Jack shouted against the wind. He was wonderfully patient and indulgent when I got into one of my moods, and I wasn't going to argue with him.

"Thanks, Jack!" I wasn't sure he heard me. I loved this place. I wanted to experience all of it.

"Long ago I stopped noticing the things around me, stopped appreciating them," he said reflectively, but loud enough for me to hear. He was leaning against a tree close behind me. "You make me feel alive on so many levels. I see the world fresh when I look at it through your eyes."

His words touched my heart, but then I remembered our mission. "If you're only giving me fifteen minutes, I'm using every one of them. Save your sweet talk for later so I can show you how much I value it."

I rushed ahead, but could hear him having no problem keeping up. "Not so fast, angel. Your wings transport you much faster than we mere mortals can move."

He was close enough to see me in the blinding snow, but stood silently so I could capture the picture of the fox who had not yet noticed my presence. It was getting colder by the minute. Jack thought I'd try to fight him, but I knew we wouldn't be able to stay even the allotted time. After the fox moved on, I stood slowly. I'd been frozen in place and it was an effort to move. Jack got close but still had to yell above the rising wind to tell me we had to head back.

I knew he was right. I lifted my hand in acknowledgment, but my lips were too frozen to reply, even though my face was almost completely covered. Everything was so new. Part of me wanted to get closer to the water in this storm. But I wasn't going to be foolish.

I turned to follow when, without warning, a bobcat leapt in front of me from its hiding place. Startled, I slipped on an icy rock and fell backwards. Although he was only a few feet away, I hit the ground so fast that Jack couldn't get to me in time to break my fall.

In the mere seconds it took for him to reach me, the snow had already started covering my supine body. Relief swept through him as I opened my eyes.

"Do you hurt anywhere?"

"Other than my pride? I'm feeling a little winded, but I've known worse." I tried to make light of it. "If you can help me up, I'll come with you meekly. And you'd better enjoy that, because it's the last time you'll ever hear me say it."

"You can't be *too* hurt, your tongue is still sharp." Gently he helped me to my feet. When he saw I was moving gingerly, he picked me up against my protests and carried me the short distance home. Closing the door behind him with his foot, he set me on the couch and started tearing off my clothes.

"Now is probably not the time to get rough or frisky," I teased, but when I saw the determination on his face, I fell silent. He had his clothes on the floor in seconds and had scooped me in his arms and was pulling back the covers of my bed.

"What are you doing, Jack? How can you possibly want to . . ." My voice trailed off as his piercing gaze stopped me cold.

"Nothing will get you warmer faster than body heat." He settled us under the comforter, my freezing skin against his already warming body. He rubbed my arms and back as he held me close. "What was I thinking to let you go out there? I should have my head examined," he whispered.

"I'm glad you were here, Jack. If I'd been alone, I probably would've gone by myself."

He made a noise that sounded suspiciously like a growl. Before he could reprimand me, I pledged, "I totally understand how foolish it was. You have my solemn vow I won't do something like that again, especially if I'm alone." As he rubbed life into my frozen limbs, I had what I thought was a brilliant idea.

"You've been involved in building. How much do you know about structural support?"

He smiled indulgently. "I can change a light bulb." He tucked my head under his chin to give us both more body heat.

"No, listen. You know how they have a 'crow's nest' on a pirate ship? Well maybe Daddy could build one off the loft."

I felt his chest rumble and leaned up on an elbow to look at him. He immediately pulled me back to his chest as I continued.

"We could make it out of glass with a small, sealable opening. That way I'd be able to put my lens out of the opening without having to face the raw elements that hit so quickly at this elevation. What do you think of *that* idea, Jack?"

Jack wasn't going to be pulled into the discussion. His eyes were closed. I was fully cocooned in his arms, and he lay silently with the hint of a smile on his face.

"I love the way you indulge me," I teased. His smile was like a pat on the head, telling me to be a good girl and get some rest.

As warmth revisited my body, sleep overtook me. Jack's body temperature had risen as well, and I was where I loved to be, securely wrapped in his arms. My last conscious thought was telling him I loved him. I didn't care anymore. He was a vital part of my existence, and I needed to say the words.

I don't know how long I'd been asleep when he started kissing me awake. I could feel his arousal against my leg. How quickly things can change . . . one minute I'm frozen in the snow, then I'm being seduced in a warm bed by my very own rescuer.

"In my whole life I didn't know you could feel this way about someone," he said. "I keep thinking about our cliff, wanting to meet you there, that place only you and I can visit in the quiet of our mind. I want you like I've never had you."

Even if he hadn't been touching me, his words would have stirred me to passion. I rolled on top of him, kissing him as though my life depended on it. I wanted to see him, to look at his face that was so pleasing to me as I took him inside me, as I rocked over him, sending unimaginable sensations into every pore in my body.

"How do you want me, Jack? What can I do to bring you pleasure? What do you see when you close your eyes and imagine this?"

In short, breathless words, he guided me, touched me, bringing us both to the brink. Just as we reached our climax, the thunder started rumbling down the side of the mountain. Sated, Jack ran his hands through my hair, bringing my lips down to meet his.

"Thundersnow," I said, nuzzling his neck. "Did you know that one of the reasons it rumbles like it does is because the snow works as a sound suppressor? All of the reverberation is enclosed in a small space."

Holding my face with both hands he teased, "A valuable science lesson, no doubt." His voice grew more tender, "Whenever I hear thundersnow, I'll think of this moment."

"So tell me, you old dog, have you got something going on with Morning Sun?"

The blush I'd come to love crept up Sam's neck to his cheeks and exploded in a riot of color above his beard.

"You wanting some coffee this morning?"

"Spill the beans. You're not getting away with your diversionary tactics again. Tell me, tell me, give it up."

"What in the gall darn blazes makes you think something's going on with me and that old woman?"

"How about that I know it was Morning Sun who was in your back room that day? How about I saw her car in your driveway on my way home from Boulder? How about she sat in the front row of your award ceremony and looked at you with puppy dog eyes? How about when . . ."

"All right, all right. But don't go telling no one. A man's gotta do what a man's gotta do. She ain't the prettiest thing I ever laid eyes on, but she takes good care of me, and she fixes a wicked pot of chili. It's a nice change to have someone to warm my bed."

"I'm so happy for you. But you tell her if she does you wrong, she'll have to answer to me."

"Well, ain't you a protective little piece of goods? I think I like that."

Coming home later, I called, "Hey, Jack, I was right!"

"You usually are. What specifically are you talking about?" he asked as I set my bag on the counter.

"Sam *is* involved with Morning Sun! He seems content. That makes *me* happy for him."

"Good for him. Now don't badger him about it. He'll come around to letting us in on his situation over time. Let him set the pace."

"He was so cute when I asked him. Blushed redder than if he'd been out in the sun all day."

"The whole time I've been here, I've never known him to be involved with anyone. 'Course I wouldn't know he was involved with *her* if you hadn't gone snooping around."

Laughing, I said, "I have some absolutely wretched news to share with you." I put my head against his back and my arms around his waist.

"Sounds serious, angel," he said, turning and leaning against the counter as he folded me into his arms. "What's this tragedy that's about to befall?"

"I'm leaving you." His body stilled and his breathing slowed.

"Talk to me," he said quietly, not moving.

"It feels like a tragedy to me," I lamented, only half teasing. "I have to be gone for a few days. I have a multi-million dollar client coming to town, and I've been asked to speak at a convention in _"

"Please don't ever do that again," he said as his arms tightened. "Leaving's not something we tease about. I've found I rather like having you around." He absently ran his fingers through my hair, curling the end around his finger, his unaware-but-tender habit I'd come to love.

I pulled away and looked at his lovable face that was such a part of me. "Really?"

He seemed to focus, kissed me on the cheek, and walked back to the sink. "Of course. I've never had pancakes that even approach how delectable yours are. Sam's don't hold a candle. Can't imagine what I'd do without them."

"You brat." I rolled up the dishtowel to pop him, but he was quicker and grabbed it before the snap hit. He kissed me senseless.

"Now, tell me where you're going . . . when, where, how long? Maybe I can get some work done while you're gone."

"What were we talking about?" I asked, coming out of the fog of his kiss.

"That seems to be a surefire way to get you to stop talking. I'll have to remember it. Now tell me about your plans." He rubbed his finger tenderly over my lips, then turned back to the dishes. We spent the next fifteen minutes talking about my four days away, how he would, of course, take care of the place, and what I'd be doing.

"Do you enjoy speaking in front of an audience? The teaching?"

"I love sharing what I know," I replied honestly. "I love helping make people better at what they do. I've done it long enough I don't think about it anymore. In some form or another, I've been around the business all my life."

"You've got such a giving spirit. I'd love to sit in on one of your lectures sometime. But I'm not up for hitting Vegas this week, even if it's to see you wow the crowds."

"What a delightful idea, Jack, let's plan on it. Maybe next time. Denver's gonna be a ball buster for the first thirty-six hours, then I fly out, meet with the organizers, spend the day at the conference, then fly back the following day. Won't be a lot of down time, but I would love it if we could take a trip together someday."

"We'll be friends forever, little one. There'll be plenty of time."

Speechless, I stood watching him. He didn't appear to be conscious of what he'd said – or how his simple words could rock my world.

Our lovemaking that night was new, unique, intense.

"Is it my imagination, or do we keep getting better at this?" I asked as I lay back to catch my breath.

"Your imagination is pretty spectacular, but there's no question we're perfecting the art."

"Fine tuning - not a bad way to spend an evening," I teased. I was struck by the coming days. "I can't bear the thought of going."

"Hush, it'll be over before you know it. It'll do you good to get back in your world, see some friends, be reminded of how vibrant you are. It'll all work out, I promise."

"How is it you always know the right thing to say? But you're right. I know it'll be okay. I'm just whining."

"Ah, my favorite." He took my face and kissed me tenderly.

"It'll be good for both of us. I've got things to do I can't seem to get done with you underfoot all the time."

I wasn't stung. I loved this time afterwards, knowing we were as close as two people could be and not wanting it to end.

"There's no question the sex is the best ever," I said, "but more than anything, I've never known a friendship like ours. I can't imagine *liking* anyone as much as I like you." I gave a final yawn before falling into a restful sleep in his arms.

The following morning was comfortably rushed, and there was enough to do to prepare for going away for a few days I didn't think about the leaving.

"I'll be so busy there won't be a lot of down time, but you'd better keep in touch with me, Mr. Franklin."

"It's a deal," he said, leaning in the car door to give me a farewell kiss. "Shall I send you salacious videos while you're gone so you don't forget what I look like?"

"Delightful thought!" I called after him, laughing and intrigued at the same time.

Chapter Twelve

CALLIE'S EYRIE

*a*s expected, the day was full and rewarding. My clients found a house and wanted to make an offer. I called Marge.

"Hey, I'm heading back to the office. Can you get the paperwork started on 736 Maple in Cherry Creek before I get back? The Baldwins want to make an offer to close in six weeks."

"Sure, thing, Callie. Are they coming in with you now?"

"They're in their own car and plan to stop to get something to eat, then they'll head over, so we have a little time. I'll be there in about twenty."

As I pulled into the parking lot of the office, I noticed I'd missed several texts. My smile was evident as I saw they were all from Jack. There was a definite theme to the thread.

'Missing you. I'll have to think of something special to do for you when you get back.'

'Did I mention I want you right now? Slow, hard, deep, wet, gentle, easy? Last night was beyond words. It will go in a pocket of lifetime memories. Let's do it again soon.'

'You are so sexy to me. I can't believe the chemistry between us on so many levels - mental, physical, emotional. I sure like you, Callie Weston.'

'You've always been able to pleasure me with just a thought, just a word. I want to touch you all the time. I always want my mouth on you. I want you to burn for me the way I'm always on fire for you.'

'Since the day I met you, I've wanted you to be aware of me.'

When I'd asked him to keep in touch, I had no idea how much fun this quiet exchange might be.

'Who IS this?'

Do I need to show you to remind you?

'OMG - if the Baldwins weren't going to be here soon, I'd put the car in reverse and head home. You'd better be able to take care of that promise when I get back.'

When I can't take care of that promise, I'll be six feet under.

'I'm so crazy about you, Jack. Thank you for bringing such light and strength into my life.'

You've always had your own strength. We just bring out the best in each other. We'll be friends forever. Now get back to work so I can get back to work.

'Aye aye, captain. Catch you on the flip side.'

Marge and I had a few moments of hugging and exchanging pleasantries as I arrived at my office. "It's wonderful to see you smiling again. What's his name? Looks like you might be laying some ghosts to rest."

"I didn't know humans like Jack existed. Not sure my feet have touched the ground in weeks."

"I cleared my schedule for you. Let's get this contract done and then have dinner and wine and you can tell me all about him. Unless you have other plans, that is."

"Of course not. Nothing I'd rather do than catch up with you. Well, I can think of a few things," I laughed, "but if I have to be in Denver, I'm excited to spend time with you."

It took several hours, but the Baldwins came and went and the contract had been sent to the Listing Agent.

"Ready to go, Missy?" Marge said from the doorway, putting on her coat.

"Give me a minute and let me call the other agent and let him know it's been sent. It should only take me a few . . ."

Marge came in and sat down, recognizing it wasn't going to be such a quick call. Almost ten minutes later, I ended the call abruptly.

"What was that about?" Marge asked.

"I have no idea. For some reason he decided I needed to know his life story. Why do people *do* that to me?"

"It's who you've always been. I've never seen anything like it. Within five minutes of standing in line with you at the grocery store or movie theater, you know their entire life story without ever asking. No one would even think of opening up to me like that. I've always thought it was strange – and sweet."

Throughout the day and evening, it would bring a smile to my heart when I heard the chime of a new message.

I love being in you. Throbbing gently, no pushing, just the natural pulse of a man inside the woman he loves. Feeling my heart beating inside you.

I'd love to be swollen and hard, moving inside you. You around me as your tightness softens into wet openness.

Here's something I've been thinking about. Do you love the idea of bringing each other to intense levels, then stopping and holding with our natural throbs? No action from either of us. Just enjoying the feeling of being one. I love that thought.

Our offer had been accepted and Marge and I were sitting at a popular restaurant waiting for our food. We toasted to a good day when the phone chimed.

"He certainly seems persistent," said Marge.

"I'm sorry, Marge. He seems determined," I laughed as I looked at my phone.

I want you to know what you do to me. Do you know I physically ache for you? Just that slight subtle feeling that doesn't go away. Hard to describe, but always there.

"What is it?" Marge asked.

Coming out of my haze, I focused and said, "Sometimes I'm

overwhelmed at the depth of feeling between us. I had no idea people could feel this way about each other. I've certainly never experienced anything like it. It's like I'm alive for the first time in my life. And every day, he reinforces it, keeps making me love him more."

Touching my hand, Marge said, "I couldn't be happier for you. You've been so single minded for so long, I despaired you would waste your youth chasing deals and clients and teaching and miss out on love."

"Looks like I'm making up for lost time. Thanks for being so understanding. Who knew something so wonderful could come out of something as ugly as Jason? If it hadn't been for him, I never would have gone up there. So I guess there is *that* to thank him for."

"I can't even think about him without my blood boiling," Marge said. "I'm so glad he's behind bars. Do you ever think about what happens when he gets out?"

"Absolutely not. And I don't want you to think about him, either. I couldn't have made it without you. You were my strength and my sanity when I was sure I was losing my mind."

"It's easy to see how you thought that, knowing there's no way anyone could get in, then coming home and things being just *slightly* different. Would've made anyone crazy."

"Thank you for that, but thank God it's behind us. As strong as I am, I can't imagine what happens to women when they don't have the support system I did. I'm so glad it's over."

"Yeah, let's concentrate on this wonderful thing that came out of it. Tell me about him."

"I feel like I'm the first person to ever have been in love. Sometimes I think no one could have felt this way before because how could anything get accomplished if you walked around with your head in the clouds?"

"You deserve it. I can't wait to meet this paragon," she laughed. We talked for another half hour, then headed back to Marge's house.

"I have an early flight. I plan on polishing my speech for tomorrow, then go to bed. Thank you for everything. I don't know what I would've done without you. You've always been there for me."

"You know you're like one of my own. It's not just my job. You're family and you know it."

"I'll be gone before you wake up. I'll leave the contract in your capable hands for the next few days. You know how to reach me if you need me."

As I settled on the bed with my laptop, the phone chimed.

If you continue to ignore me, I may have to resort to drastic measures.

'Oh, yeah? What measures are we talking about?'

There you are! It's been a long day without you. Full of so many conflicting emotions and overlapping circles. I've missed you.

'I'm not going anywhere except to Vegas tomorrow and then back into your arms. I'll be back before you know it.'

I know I've been filtering with you. There's so much wrapped up in my brain about us, and there's a certain anxiety.

'What kind of anxiety?'

We'll talk when you get back. I always want you, always need you. You're my fire. You heal me on so many levels even I don't understand.

His words were silken. I couldn't believe this was the hard, intense stranger I'd met a few months ago. There was such passion in him. He'd been holed up way too long.

If it exists in my life, it involves you.

'I love your words, Jack. They enchant me. Make me feel like you're here.'

You're my thunder and lightning.

'I have to get up in less than six hours to catch a plane. I will love you while I'm gone, and love you even more when I see you again.'

Good night. Let me know when you get there.

The plane trip the following day was turbulent. I was queasy from the flight, I felt whiny, and all I wanted to do was go home. It was the first time in memory I wasn't excited about the coming presentation. I wanted to be done. I'd never had anyone at home waiting before, but it was a powerful pull. I liked it.

Speeches and meetings and conferences had me exhausted by the time I got to my room that night. Tired to the bone and not interested in meeting the organizers for dinner, I collapsed into blissful sleep, knowing I didn't even have to set an alarm for the following morning because my flight wasn't until afternoon.

Several people who wanted to talk about some issues I'd raised interrupted my leisurely breakfast. My food grew cold, my book unread, and finally I politely excused myself to finish packing.

I can't wait to see your face.

The text from Jack brought me back to reality, and how quickly he had come to define that place.

'Then we can sit and stare at each other since I think you're the handsomest thing in my world.'

Since I'm not defined by my looks, it's a good thing we'll be able to find other ways to occupy ourselves, right?

'What a sly-tongued devil you are, Mr. Franklin.'

My sly tongue misses you a lot. What time will you be here?

'Plane gets in about 3:30. If I'm lucky and can slip thru rush hour, I should be home by 7, give or take a half hour.'

I'll be waiting at attention for your arrival.

'Mmmmm . . . the possibilities, Jack, the possibilities. Heading to the airport. Will call when I land.'

"WE'VE GOT ABOUT EIGHT HOURS TO HAVE THIS PROJECT DONE AND everything cleared out," Jack called to the workmen. "I'll grab lunch. Keep working 'til I get back, then you can take a break."

As Jack was leaving to get food, Charles drove up. After a welcoming hug, Charles said, "I came up to see how things are going, make sure it'll be done before she gets back. I also wanted to see what it actually looks like. Sounded fascinating."

"Good to see you, old man. It's coming along well. Head to town with me and I'll show you around when we get back."

"Love what you're doing, Jack. Callie will be so surprised."

"It was either this or have her kill herself when the snows fall. You sure raised a butt-headed daughter."

"Takes after her mother. You don't seem to mind?" Charles was looking for answers.

"No, I don't mind. I've become pretty fond of your little urchin."

They picked up a pack of burgers and fries from the Pioneer Inn. It was good Callie would be going straight home before she stopped anywhere in town because Candice's boyfriend was on the work crew. Word would be everywhere in no time. It was the way of life in a small town. When they left the Pioneer Inn, they stopped at Dam Liquor to pick up beer, then headed back.

"She tough, but she's got a heart of gold. And you'd best not forget who her father is."

Jack patted Charles on the back as they headed into the house. "I assure you, I'm not likely to forget."

"Take a break, guys," Jack called out. The men headed into the kitchen while Jack showed Charles the work that was almost finished.

"I've never seen anyone with an imagination like yours. Callie will be thrilled with your concept. But more importantly, I know my little girl. She doesn't take anything for granted. She'll be moved beyond measure that someone cared enough to do something like this for her. Lotta brownie points your little addition will garner."

"It was her idea. I just knew how to get it done."

After several companionable hours, Charles and all of the workmen were finally done and gone. Everything was in order, and Jack was surprised how much he'd missed Callie, even though she'd only been gone a few days. He felt like a teenager as he lit candles and put the finishing touches on a simple dinner of grilled chicken with a fresh salad.

Chapter Thirteen

CHESS SET

*W*hen I walked through the door, Jack and I stood for a few moments just looking at each other. I set my suitcase down and looked around. The table was set, candles lit, and wonderful smells had my stomach growling.

"You did all this for me?" I asked, deeply touched by his thoughtfulness.

"I missed you," he said, wrapping me against him. "I needed something to occupy my time while I waited for you to get back."

"Are you real? Can I keep you?" We laughed until our lips met. Then there was nothing funny anymore, only the passion that continually flared between us.

"Let me take care of one physical need before we start working on satisfying another," he said. "Go wash up. I'll get the food on the table."

Dinner was intimate, romantic, delicious. I told him about my conference and how different it was because this time, all I wanted was to get home. When we finished, Jack poured a second glass of wine and said, "Would you like to continue this discussion in front of the fire? I've been stoking it all evening."

"Which fire have you been stoking?"

"Don't you understand yet? The other fire takes care of itself. That fire is always stoked. All I need to do is think about you and I'm hot again."

That night I learned what it truly meant to make love to someone. The emotion involved, the passion, the feeling of being one. If this is what his response would be when I'd been gone for a few days, I'd have to leave more often.

As the sun rose the following morning, Jack woke me with a steaming cup of coffee.

"Wake up, little one. I have something I want you to see."

"What are you doing? How can you possibly be up so early after last night?"

"The sun's coming up, the snow is falling, and I have something to show you."

His excitement was infectious. After a stretch and a yawn, I put my feet over the side of the bed and took the proffered cup. "Give me just a few. I'll throw on some clothes and be right with you."

Ten minutes later, feeling almost human, Jack was waiting for me. He took my hand and said, "Come on, come on. I want you to see this."

"All right, all right. You said that. Show me."

He led me toward the back of the house. "Wait, Jack. It's snowing. Neither one of us is dressed to go outside."

"Trust me. You don't need to be bundled up."

As we turned into the back hallway where there had once been a wall, there was now a spiral staircase. I felt a tilting of my reality.

"I don't understand?" I looked at Jack, then looked around the transformed area.

"You don't need to understand yet. Just trust."

I stepped on the first rung. "This is surreal. Are you coming?" I asked, not sure whether or not to be excited. "Did you slip something into my coffee? Have we entered another dimension in space?"

Patting me gently on the butt, Jack laughed and said, "Go on, go on."

Hearing the excitement in his voice, I made the tentative first steps. As I rounded the final curve, there was an enclosed, glassed-in platform that allowed me a view of the reservoir, the town, and the mountains to the west.

Incredulous, not totally grasping the situation, I searched his face for some sort of explanation. His face was engaging. "You're the one who mentioned the crow's nest on a ship. I've been thinking of it and wondering what it would look like. An eagle is more appealing than a crow. 'Eyrie' is an eagle's nest that's often built into the side of a rock formation high above everything else.

"I called your dad when I found out you were leaving town. He made the arrangements. The crew worked around the clock to have it done before you got back. Welcome to *Callie's Eyrie*."

"I love the name!"

He showed me an almost invisible handle that opened a long, narrow window. "There are three of these on the front, and three on the west side. When the weather's bad, you'll be able to open any one of them, your lens will fit through with plenty of room to maneuver, and you won't have to be outside risking your life."

I stood motionless, overwhelmed.

"It's designed so there aren't many places east or north or west that your lens won't be able to capture. Since you can't get shots to the south on this side of the mountain anyway, it was the best I could do."

"The best you could do?" I asked, tears brimming.

"What is it? Aren't you thrilled?"

"Thrilled? I can hardly breathe. Oh, my God, Jack. There doesn't exist a word for what I am."

After a few minutes watching the falling snow, warm and secure in each other's arms, he whispered gently, "You inspire me to greatness. You encourage me in ways I didn't know I wanted to be encouraged. My desire was to do something nice for you, bring you pleasure. Well, more pleasure than what I do for you most mornings in your bed."

We laughed, but I was bursting. I disentangled myself and said, "Wait here," and rushed to get my equipment.

Standing on the stairway with camera in hand, I took pictures of Jack above me, looking out over the reservoir. He smiled down at me as I captured the essence of him. "I'm so glad you like it," he smiled. "I was afraid you'd think I was trying to clip your wings."

"You can't be serious?" I said, coming up next to him. "If I live to be a hundred, this will be the single most exquisite moment in my life. This is protection, not clipping my wings."

Opening the carefully disguised windows, I was lost in what was happening in the design, the functionality, the excitement. "I'm speechless."

"Let me show you some of its secrets." There were switches that opened and closed the floor access, that adjusted lighting, that adjusted temperature.

"I've been around building and design a long time, Jack. I can't imagine the work and man-hours that went into something like this, much less getting the materials up here and finding the workers to get it done. I can't wrap my brain around it."

"Your dad and I talked, he loved the idea. I'd been working on the plans since the first time you mentioned it, just waiting for a few days when you weren't around to be able to get it done. I called in some favors . . . voila."

The rest of the day passed blissfully. I kept asking questions as more logistics occurred to me.

"How in the world did you get all the debris out of here?"

"Each of the guys had their truck. They hauled it when they left."

"Where did you find electricians and carpenters and glass installers on such short notice?"

"I told you. I'm a Jack of all Trades. I've been in the business a long time. Your dad sent his crew and I called in some favors."

"I never knew the heart had this capacity to expand. If I died right this minute, I wonder if heaven could be more wonderful?"

"After I've gone to all this work, you better not die right now," he teased.

"Isn't it amazing that we've been in the same type of business all these years, both of us between Denver and Boulder, and we didn't run into each other until we ran away to an obscure mountain town with little more than a thousand people?"

"I've known about you for a while. Your father's pretty proud of you."

"Yeah, I'm all he has, so he obsesses and tends to see my accomplishments like he's the only parent whose child has ever succeeded."

"I didn't know your mother, but I know your dad is one of the finest men I've known. You're both pretty lucky."

"Thank you, I think so too."

"Before it gets too bad out there, I need to run home and take care of a few things. I've been a little preoccupied the past few days. They're calling for several feet of snow, so I want to make sure things are secure."

"Hey! Do you realize I've never seen your place? Can I tag along?"

"Soon. Right now, would you mind heading into town, grab some groceries in case we have to hole up for more than a day or two, and check on Sam? I'll meet you back here?"

"Wouldn't that be wonderful, not being able to leave for a few days? Maybe I'll pick up a deck of cards so we have something to do to pass the time," I teased as I headed off to town.

"What brings you down here as the snow starts to fly? I thought you'd be all cozied up with appreciation this morning. Sure was a special thing he did."

"It hasn't sunk in yet. Not just what it is, but that he thought of it, that he did it. I'm blown away."

"Yeah, your pa was pretty tickled."

"You saw my dad?"

"Sure. He came up to see what all the fuss were about, see how Jack Franklin was looking out for his little girl. Yep, he was one proud papa."

"I know Jack said my dad was in on it, but it hadn't actually occurred to me he was here. It's strange to think that while I was gone for a few days, all of this was taking place. Another little treasure to put in the box to open at a later time."

"Ain't none of us don't have mighty strong feelings for you, Missy. You do so much for all the town folk, helping out Griz, taking Ms. Jenny to the doc when she fell, buying groceries for Farley when he were sick, helping me out around here without even being aware you're doing it. You bring us lotsa sunshine, ain't many that don't know you're family."

"Thank you, Sam. Being here has had me feeling emotions I never knew existed."

I caught a glance out the window as the ground was turning white. "I came down to check on you and get some supplies. You closing up?"

"Like a little mother hen. Get on with you now and get what you need. I'll be heading out in a few. Folks keep showing up for a cooked meal to take home or I woulda been done a long time ago."

"Do you need anything? Can I drop it off on my way up?"

"Nah, appreciate it, but I'm all stocked up. This one's supposed to be a Nor'easter, so get on outta here."

"Will do. Love you, Sam."

"You sure can make me blush. Get on with you . . ."

There was a spring to my step as I got supplies for a few days. Normally prepared, I hadn't replenished because I'd known I wouldn't be around, but it was a rush knowing Jack and I would be spending at least the next twenty-four hours together.

I SET THE GROCERIES ON THE COUNTER NEXT TO AN ALLURING BOX THAT appeared to have been carved from burled black walnut.

"What's this?" I asked as Jack was loading the bin with firewood.

"A little something I thought might help us pass the time if we get bored."

"Yeah, like that's gonna happen," I smiled. "May I open it?"

"Be my guest."

What was inside was an exquisite chess set. "I'm almost afraid to touch them," I said reverently, removing a Knight from its specially designed resting place. "Look at the hair on the horses head. It's so intricate and wavy. The Queen is magnificent. I've never seen anything like them. Where did you find them?"

"I made them. They're carved from black walnut and basswood. The board's made out of the same woods," he said, sliding it out of its hiding place. "Are you always this sentimental?" he teased, seeing my expression.

"Where'd you get the idea for them?"

"It's been just me and the carnival of my mind for so long, kinda like Scott down at the Carousel. They didn't take me twenty-five years, but I had an advantage that mine were much smaller."

I reverently touched the pieces. "This isn't about the amazing talent or the patience it would take, it's about the heart. Once again, I can't explain how they make me feel. They're so real, as if they have their own personalities."

Pleased with my response, he pulled me close. "We'll play after dinner. If you don't know how, I'll teach you."

"My dad and I used to play when my mom was sick. We'd sit in her room for hours, quietly, just to be there with her. Chess is a fond memory."

We spent hours playing that night.

"Best two outta three?" he asked, after each of us had won thoroughly enjoyable games.

"The snow is piling up and it's almost midnight," I said, no longer able to control my yawns. "Shall we let the winner be decided tomorrow? It's not like we're going anywhere."

"We're always on the same page. Tomorrow it is."

Falling asleep in his arms, I was sure I'd never been more content. "I love you, Jack Franklin," I whispered as my last conscious thought. He squeezed me in acknowledgment.

The snowflakes were falling furiously as the sun sent rays playing across the room. Jack was under the covers, tenderly fondling my nipple with his tongue.

"Is there anything you don't do perfectly?" I asked, still mostly asleep.

"I'm not sure. But let me know if you find something."

I could feel his smile against my chest with his morning growth of beard, feel his hardness against my leg. I wanted to grind against him, but I also wanted to be still, to enjoy. "I have just enough stubble to make you aware. Let me know if it's too rough."

But I wasn't listening. I was too busy enjoying.

Chapter Fourteen

STALKER ON THE LOOSE

"*H*ave you ever noticed how affectionate you are after we've made love?" Jack said as we worked companionably in the kitchen. "Not just right after, but all day. It's endearing."

"Thanks. Does that mean I'm better than a cigarette afterwards?"

He touched my face, covering my lips with his. "Even my lips miss you when you're not moving in sync with them."

"I'm always so aware of you afterwards." I was surprised he could still make me blush. "It's so fun, the tease mode we get into. In my dreams, I couldn't have imagined you to conjure you up."

"You're so much better than I deserve. It's hard to explain what you do to me."

Our days were full of captivating hours, our nights overflowed with magic. One morning after the snows melted, I found a letter on the kitchen counter. His handwriting was precise and perfectly formed, and my heart raced as I poured a cup of coffee to read his missive.

Friend of my heart - No matter where I am, you're with me. You're so much a part of me, I don't know where I end and you begin. I can't seem to be able to adequately express what I want to tell you.

The first night you walked into Sam's place, I felt my world shift. I didn't want to be aware of anyone like I was at that moment, but there you stood. Alarms went off, and I knew in that instant my life had been altered. For a while I fought the inevitable. Now I fight the feelings of fear that I've imagined you.

Over the months, I've seen you make me a better person. I never considered I was empty until you filled me. Last night when you put your hand against mine, I thought it was symbolic how we fit each other — where I have valleys, you fill me. Where I have peaks, I fill your valleys.

I love your heart. In my world, you are the most stunning human I know. You not only rock me with your physical beauty, but your spirit mesmerizes me.

My purpose is only to express what I don't think I've adequately conveyed - I wasn't living before you came into my life.

Knowing Jack had appointments most of the day, I sent him a text: *I will cherish this note forever. I'll never tire of hearing your words. From the bottom of my heart, thank you.*

His familiar ding sounded ten minutes later. 'You are my world.'

BUSINESS WAS GREAT, BUT I WAS TIRED OF THE HOURS I'D BEEN working in Denver. I'd recently turned thirty and was finding the things I thought I wanted paled in comparison to the time I was spending here. It wasn't only Jack, but also the people who inhabited this pleasant village, the carefree way of life. I loved being part of it.

Needing a break from contracts and negotiations, I grabbed my camera and made sure I was well equipped with winter gear, even though the weather this morning was nice. I headed up to Lefthand Canyon, a place I hadn't yet visited. Parking my car at the trail-head, I texted Jack.

Going up to Lefthand and heading toward Fireman Hill. If you don't have anything better to do with your time, maybe we can reconnoiter at my place later. Should be back just after sunset.

As I was getting my camera bag out of the back seat, his familiar ring indicated a response.

As long as you don't mind a fully aroused, naked man lying on your couch when you walk in the door, plan on me being there.

With a snap in my step, I set off to film this enclave that was popular with ATVs, determined to make it as far as I could to the top. I heard you could see not only the entire Front Range from there, but also downtown Boulder.

The lack of noise and the sense of serenity were tangible. I loved the solitude. I'd walked several miles up the trail when I saw a huge boulder at the edge of the woods. The temperature was falling fast, and I decided to climb to the top of the rock to have a bite to eat and catch the majesty of the storm that now appeared to be coming in over the ridge.

The boulder was considerably larger than it appeared from a distance. I circled to see if I could gain a foothold. I was on the side, examining it to see if I could climb it if I threw my equipment up first, when I saw someone approaching from the path I'd just traveled.

Dammit. I'd have to sit it out for a bit to allow him to pass. Not only did I not want him in my photos, I also didn't want to alert anyone to my presence since I was here by myself. I set the bag on the ground and pulled out my camera. Something registered in my spine that things weren't right. What was it that was setting off my internal alarm? The approaching stranger walked with a degree of familiarity. Silently putting on my telephoto lens, I stayed as much behind the rock as possible while training my lens on the encroacher.

Dear God in heaven, it was Jason! I couldn't move from my hiding place without alerting him to my presence, but it didn't matter, I was frozen to this spot. I pulled out my phone to text Jack, but I no longer had cell service. I shot a few photos of Jason, just in case, and quietly packed my equipment and waited.

He was walking slowly. I was sure he'd be able to hear the desperate beat of my heart. It was deafening in my ears, and I wondered if I'd pass out from the frantic flow of blood through my veins. No! I was stronger and smarter and better than I'd ever been, and he would not win.

I maneuvered to the back side of the rock as he drew closer. His footsteps were even louder than the roar of my pulse, and I edged back again as he came within yards of my hiding place. Switching sides of my stone protection as he passed, he didn't appear to be aware of me as the sound of his footfalls grew fainter.

It was now freezing and there were huge flakes in the air. I knew I had to make a move. I couldn't risk opening my case to get my jacket, so I slowly edged my way to the tree line. As I got behind a tree, I heard a twig snap.

Frantic, I nearly cried out in relief when I realized I'd stepped on a small branch. Oh, God, please don't let him have heard. I waited, but the howl of the wind drowned out any sound it may have carried. It appeared safe to run, so I did.

Staying inside the line of trees, I ran as fast as I could through the brush. I'd slow down every now and then to look, but he hadn't come over the hill, and the snow was falling in earnest. Any of my footprints that might have been left would be easily obliterated with the fast-approaching storm.

I stayed behind the tree closest to my car until I was sure I could make it quickly and undetected to the driver's door. Keys at the ready, no one near, I made a dash for it. There was only one other car in the lot, a car parked next to mine. I assumed Jason had rented one to remain undetected.

How had he known I was here? Did he know where I was living? Why hadn't they told me he'd been released? Would he follow me when he made it back to the car? Hands shaking from the cold and an adrenaline rush, I pulled the revolver out of my glove box, contemplating whether or not to shoot his gas tank.

Backing out of the parking space, I looked around anxiously, searching to make sure he wasn't near.

Fearful that a shot would bring him running, I thought desperately of something else I could do to slow him down. This was not going to be a light storm, and I needed to get out of here. Pausing only a fraction of a minute, I grabbed a knife from the console. Daddy always said, "Never bring a knife to a gunfight, but if you don't have a gun, make sure you have a knife." Since meeting Jason, I carried both.

He was nowhere to be seen. I knelt beside the back of his car on the cold, wet gravel. Gripping the handle tightly, I raised both hands above my head and shoved it with every ounce of terrified strength I possessed into his rear passenger tire.

From the comfort of my front seat, feeling somehow victorious, it took only a minute for me to watch the rear of his car sag as the tire deflated. Now he would at least be able to get warm in his car, but it would slow him enough for me to get to safety. I took a picture of the license plate.

The ground was getting thick with snow and sticking to the untraveled roads that led to Nederland. This storm was going to be one for the records, and they hadn't even been talking about it. The random thought occurred to me that there weren't many professions, other than Meteorology, where you could be so wrong so often and still get paid for your work.

I was being careless with my speed and slowed as much as my racing heart would allow. I wanted Jack. I knew once I was in the familiar, I'd be safe. What should have taken twenty minutes took well over an hour. Images of what might have happened had I not seen Jason first took hold in my brain, making me dizzy.

It was my intention to go straight home but I saw Jack's car as I sped past the diner. My thoughts shot in all directions, my breathing coming in small gasps. I was gripping the steering wheel so tightly my hands were locked in place.

I needed Jack to tell me it was going to be all right, needed his sanity as I felt my world tilting. The bell jangled and I saw them both standing there, just as they had been that first night. Jason couldn't hurt me now.

"We were coming to look for you. You weren't answering your . . . what's the matter, Callie? What happened?" Jack said, taking me by the shoulders.

Examining my face, he said, "Are you cold? Why are you shaking like that? What happened?"

"I'll get her a blanket," Sam said, and was immediately unfolding one, wrapping it around me.

"He's here. He found me."

They exchanged looks but neither needed to ask who 'he' was. They knew.

"Did he touch you? Did he hurt you?"

"No. He didn't see me. I was isolated in the middle of nowhere, and there he was. I hid until he passed." I told them the story as coherently as possible, all the while being soothed and petted by Jack.

"Did you see him as you left?" asked Sam, angry and pulling a shotgun from behind the counter.

"No, Sam. He hadn't made it back to the car when I left. There was no sign of him. But he didn't touch me. You can't go threatening him with a gun."

"I don't plan on putting a bullet in his sorry ass . . . at least not yet. But I sure will put the fear a God in him. I ain't never gonna let nobody put that look on my pun'kin's face again . . . never."

"Tell us exactly where he was. If he was the only one there, we should be able to follow his tracks."

"Better yet, I'll show you."

Sam and Jack looked at each other and then at me. "No way" and "Absolutely not" came out simultaneously.

"Morning Sun's on her way to watch the shop. She was coming this way because we was gonna look for you. We'll head out, you stay here with her until we get back. Don't even think about leaving. She can skin a pole cat before it even knows it's been caught."

"You'll be safe here," Jack said, giving me a final squeeze.

"Don't go getting all mule headed. Promise me you'll stay here until we get back. I can't be worrying about your safety while we're gone."

"I promise, but you have to promise you'll be careful. I'd kill him with my bare hands if anything happened to either one of you."

"If we find him, we're gonna have a little 'come to Jesus' meeting with him."

Sam chuckled and said under his voice, "Yep, he'll find a whole heap a religion, that's for dang sure."

Morning Sun was pulling up as Jack and Sam got to the car. They spoke to her briefly, then backed out in Jack's Land Cruiser.

We'd never been around each other much, so I was nervous and excited to have time together, just us girls. We would have a common worry as we waited. She took charge, bolting the door behind her, then drawing the shades. She didn't strike me as someone who was gonna be doing a whole lot of worrying. That put me at ease.

"Take your coat off and let's make ourselves useful around here. I've wanted to do a good cleaning on this place for a long time. Ain't nobody coming in or going out for a few hours, so we might as well put our time to good use."

"I like the way you think, Morning Sun," I smiled. "What a nice way to occupy ourselves while we wait."

"Friends call me 'Sunni'," she said, running steaming water into a big bucket. "You can call me that if you want."

"I'd be honored." I took a sponge and started cleaning the wood in the back booth.

The next few hours passed in companionable silence with bursts of conversation. I told her the story of Jason and how I'd gotten here. She told me the story of how she'd raised a son single-handedly in a nearby town after her husband left her for the city lights - and a twenty-two year old girl. By the time we heard a car in the parking lot hours later, the Amber Rose was shiny and smelled like freshly squeezed lemons. I also had a new friend.

We waited in the kitchen to make sure no one would be knocking on the door. When we heard the key turn in the lock, we shared a smile of relief and headed into the seating area. Sam was genuinely surprised as he looked around.

"Woo wee," he said, letting out a whistle. "This place didn't even look this good the day I bought her."

"We'll talk about that in a few. What happened?" I asked anxiously, looking between Jack and Sam taking off their winter gear.

"Patrol shut down the roads on the back side of Boulder. Couldn't get through. It's coming down fast and furious, and I'm afraid the old son-of-a-bitch is gonna hope he has a full tank of gas to keep him warm. He won't be going anywhere with a flat tire in this mess."

"Did I do something terribly wrong?"

He looked at me like I'd taken leave of my senses. "Are you kidding? I'm so proud of you for what you did! How could you think otherwise?"

"Because part of me felt like a chicken for not confronting him. I was seriously afraid I'd shoot him, and that would've caused so many other problems. He's definitely not worth the trouble *that* would cause in my life."

"Listen, sugar," interjected Morning Sun. "A smart person figures out a way to *avoid* a fight, not see if you can be the victor *in* one. There's no glory in being dead because you wasn't strong enough to win in a fight with an angry man."

"She's absolutely right," Jack said, touching my face. "It would've been pure foolishness to confront him in the middle of nowhere."

"Downright crazy," said Sam.

"Okay, okay. I just want it to be over."

"You got all us now," Sam said, inclining his head toward the other two. "Ain't one person that's gonna harm a hair on your head and live to tell about it."

"I'll take her on home, Sam, Sunni." Jack nodded at both of

them as he led me to the car.

"Let's take your car," Jack said, "just in case. Don't want it sitting here on this busy street for anyone to see. Not that it won't be days before anyone will be able to dig their way out."

"Great idea. Thanks for doing the thinking for me. I'm afraid my brain feels like mush."

"You're entitled. As soon as we walk in the door at your house, I want you to hop in the pond. You're shivering again."

I leaned over and put my head on his shoulder. "I can't imagine life without you, Jack Franklin," I said, yawning. "From the bottom of my heart, I'm so thankful for you."

Amazingly, I woke up as Jack was lifting me out of the car. "Don't you *dare!*" I said, coming awake with a start. "I'll walk. No way I'll let you carry me through the snow with all these clothes on."

"As you wish, ma'am. I'll follow along with your equipment."

More alert and protective than I'd ever seen him, Jack made sure all the doors and windows were locked. He brought me a steaming cup of tea as I soaked in the tub.

"Drink this. It'll help you sleep."

"Can't imagine I'll have a problem, but thank you for everything."

"As soon as we can get out, Sam and I will go back to where you last saw him. See if we can get some clues. I'm so proud of you for thinking to get the license number from his car. We should be able to track him down through the rental agency."

Settling into bed with my head on his shoulder, Jack leaned over to turn off the light. I saw the reflection of the revolver in the open drawer in the bedside table. I felt comforted and safe. I was asleep within seconds.

"Callie, Callie. You're okay, sweetheart. You're having a bad dream. Wake up, darling. You're okay. I'm here."

Waking with a start, I looked around. It was the middle of the night and Jack was here.

"Oh, Jack, it was awful! I knew I was going to die and never see you again. Stay with me, please."

"I'm here, little one. I'm never going to leave."

That was my last conscious thought until I heard the pans rattling. The sun was shining as I padded barefoot into the kitchen. I put my arms around his waist.

"Did you drug the tea?" I asked through a yawn.

"No. Yesterday took a lot out of you. I'm glad you were able to sleep."

"Holy cow! Do you see the snow out there? There must be at least eighteen inches, and it's *still* coming down!"

I took a cup of coffee and walked to the window. "Do you suppose I killed him by ruining his tire?"

"Don't even think such a thought again, do you hear me? Whatever happens, he deserves it. You left him a warm car, which is a lot more than I would have done. You protected yourself. It's all good."

"You aren't going to try to go back today, are you?"

"No. Can't imagine the roads will be open. It will be at least tomorrow. Even the tow truck won't be able to help him today."

"Do you think it will cool him off or piss him off more? I'm trying so hard not to be afraid, but how did he find me here? No one knows I'm here but Daddy and Marge, and I guarantee neither one of *them* told him."

"Who knows? Maybe he saw you one day and followed you from Denver. We don't have any way of knowing. What I *do* know is he won't come back here or he'll be very sorry. That's a promise."

"No question. I feel completely safe with you around. I know he can't hurt me if you're here."

"Not ever."

The day was spent playing chess and drinking hot cocoa and taking incredible pictures from *Callie's Eyrie*. I told him about my time with Sunni and he told me about trying to get around the police barricade. The night was spent in his arms, tenderly, passionately. Would I ever grow tired of this? Not in this lifetime, I was sure.

Chapter Fifteen

CLERICAL ERROR

When I woke up, he was gone. The note on the counter said, *You may not, under ANY circumstances, leave this house today. The only person you can open the door for is Sunni. Anyone else who belongs here will have a key. No exceptions. I know it will make you stir crazy, but until we have a chance to find out where he is, to talk to him, I don't want you anywhere else alone. The gun in the side drawer is loaded. I know you know how to use it. Don't hesitate if you have to. I will be in touch as soon as I can.*

P.S. You are my hero.

Stir crazy didn't begin to describe what I was going through. My imagination was wreaking havoc. I kept wanting to call or text Jack, but feared I might call at the wrong time and distract him from something important, so I stayed silent, waiting desperately for the phone to ring.

When the knock came at the door, it scared me to the roots of my hair. "It's me, honey. Open up. I brought you some lunch."

I was so excited at the prospect of not having just myself for company, I hurried to open the door for Sunni. "I'm so glad to see you! You have no idea how awful it is to wait!"

"I spent a good part of my life waiting. I *do* know how it can be.

Figured you'd be pacing and not taking care of yourself, so I closed up shop for a while and came up to try to put some meat on those scrawny bones of yours."

"Thank you! I didn't know I was hungry, but I knew I needed some company."

The fried chicken and macaroni and cheese were not a normal part of my diet, but they tasted so good I'm not sure I wasted time breathing while I ate. "That was, without a doubt, the best chicken ever," I said, wiping my hands.

"Glad you liked it. My ma got the recipe from her ma. No need to change a good thing if it ain't broke."

"Thank you, thank you, thank you. I'm going absolutely nuts. It's so nice to have you here."

"I came up to feed your bones, honey. I gotta get back down and open up shop again."

"Please let me come with you?"

"Are you kidding? And have me get skinned within an inch of my life? No way. You're gonna lock the door when I leave, and you ain't gonna answer 'til everything's clear, you hear me, young 'un?"

"Okay, okay, I'll find something to do. I've got a good book. I'll see if it's good enough to help me escape the nightmare called 'today.'"

"I ain't driving away 'til I hear the lock turn, understand?"

"Yes, ma'am, I understand." I gave her a hug and a kiss on the cheek. That seemed to surprise her, and she got a little smile as she left.

"Sam's right. You're one special young lady."

I locked the door and heard the crunch of snow under her tires. The book had better be good. I needed something powerful to pull me away from my thoughts.

Jack's familiar ding sounded. *We're fine. Not to worry. I won't be able to talk for a while, but I wanted you to know we're okay. Have no idea when we'll be home. Same rules apply – don't open the door for anyone. I'll be there when I get there. Can't be any more specific than that.*

'Where are you, Jack?'

Later. Can't explain now. ILY

'Take care of yourself or I'll hurt you even more if you don't!'

It took me a while, but I finally got into the popular new thriller. The author was one I enjoyed, and I had several hours of escape as I read of mysterious meetings in the Mohave and sabotage on the Seine. When I looked at the clock and saw that it was 5:00, my anxiety levels skyrocketed. Where could he possibly be? Why hadn't he called? Was he all right? I picked up my phone and called the Amber Rose to see if Sunni had heard from Sam.

"Not anything yet, darling. Take care of yourself. I'm sure they're fine. We woulda heard something by now from somebody if they weren't. Don't go troubling yourself. I'll let you know the minute I hear anything."

"You sure are a lot better at waiting than I am."

"Had a lot a practice. You're doing just fine, it'll be okay."

It took another hour for me to relax again. The book was, in fact, interesting enough to hold my attention. So much so that when the key turned in the lock several hours later, I jumped with fright. A weary Jack walked through the door, throwing his coat over the edge of the chair and opening his arms. I ran to him, never happier or more relieved to be engulfed in his strong embrace.

"What happened? Are you okay? Where's Sam? Where's Jason? Have you eaten? Talk to me!"

"If you'd slow down for a minute and let me catch my breath, I'd be glad to," he said affectionately.

"Okay, okay. I'll settle down. Do you want a drink?"

"No, Callie, you need to sit down."

The tone of his voice was solemn, almost frightening.

"Please tell me Sam's okay!"

"Yes, he's fine."

The firelight played across his rugged features as he took my hands and said, "He's dead. Jason is dead."

"Did you kill him, Jack?" I asked immediately, calmly.

He tilted his head. "Do you *think* I did?"

"I don't have any idea. I'm trying to figure out how I feel about him being dead, and why I wouldn't be upset if it was you who killed him."

"Well, *that's* certainly a conversation for another day, but no, I didn't kill him. He was dead when we found him."

"Oh, no! Did he freeze to death in his car? Was it *my* fault?"

"No," he said, "he never made it back to the car."

He pulled me back to lean against his chest. "When Sam and I got there, his car was parked in the same spot you described, with no sign of him anywhere. There were no footprints in the snow, the car was still piled deep, so we called the Sheriff's office.

"Seems Jason continued walking for miles past where you'd been hiding. The storm would've been much heavier by the time he decided to turn back. The police brought in helicopters to search the area.

"He was found a distance away, but very close to another trailhead. He obviously got hypothermia because there was an indication he was walking around in circles near where his body was found. Victims often have a false sense of being warm. He didn't have his shirt on when they spotted his body. He was probably dead within a few hours of when you last saw him."

"I keep waiting to feel a sense of remorse. I only feel relief. Does that make me a horrible person?"

"Of course not," he said, kissing my hair. "I'm not sure what we would've done if we'd found him. I'm glad I didn't have to find out."

"What happened after that?"

"We went to the Boulder Police Station and answered questions for a while. Sam and I told them the whole truth. I didn't want them finding pieces to the puzzle as time went on, as his family finds out, and you get implicated by association with me. We told them about your attack, about his jail time, about him following you out there the other day."

"Come to think of it, he only had a shirt on when he walked by me. As fast as that storm came in, he would've gotten cold in a hurry."

"Yeah, and because of the tire, it would've raised red flags. That's why Sam and I decided honesty would be best all the way around. There's no question the evidence points to what happened. They were satisfied with our explanation. They'll want to talk to you, but there's nothing to hide. I told them I'd bring you in tomorrow. There's absolutely nothing to worry about."

"I'm not worried. I will not, under any circumstances, let him hurt me from the grave. I feel no sorrow about him at all. I feel sorry for his brother, Mark, but other than that, nothing."

"It won't take long. I figure after you talk with the police tomorrow, there will be a lot of press coverage. Are you able to get away for a few days? I'd be happy to hop in the car and take you somewhere away from here. Maybe Santa Fe?"

"Of course I'll make the time."

"I want to go somewhere no one can find you. Somewhere we can be anonymous and blend into the woodwork and relax for a few days. It's not a long drive, and, according to the police, your trial with Jason was pretty high profile. You seem to be a popular figure not only in Denver but Boulder, as well. They knew exactly who you were, and there was definitely no love lost for Jason."

"It wouldn't have been unreasonable for them to initially think I'd had something to do with it. And why didn't they let me know?"

"Seems there was a system glitch the day he was released. He was actually not scheduled to get out for another month, but a clerical error sent him on his way."

"Can you imagine the heartache that's been caused in lives by that kind of mismanagement?"

"Not something I want to think about. Sam and I were sick to hear some of their stories about your trial and to know what you'd been through on your own. There's no way I want the press to put you in the middle of it again. And I don't want anyone tracking you down here. It would ruin the peace and quiet you've worked so hard to establish. It made me admire you all the more to find out just a small part of what you'd been through, and to see what an amazing woman ended up on the other side."

TRUE TO HIS WORD, JACK WHISKED ME AWAY TO A BEAUTIFUL Southwestern vacation. The interrogation by the Boulder Police was painless and routine. There was no glimmer of suspicion as to the facts of how Jason died, and they encouraged Jack to get me out of town for at least a week. We stayed at a hacienda in Taos for a few days, soaking up the sun. We spent several days at a quaint Inn off the Plaza in Santa Fe, visiting art galleries, wandering stores, and an entire day at The Nirvana Spa being pampered. There was a day trip to a National Park, and a full day exploring the surrounding areas of Santa Fe.

It had been a dream of a time, and I felt no guilt in the face of this tragedy. Both of us knew it was time to return as we lay in bed that morning.

"Are you ready to go?" he asked quietly, curling my hair around the tip of his finger.

"I love our life in Nederland. This trip has been what will become one of my fondest memories, but there has been a huge weight lifted not having to worry about Jason ever again. By the time we get back it will be yesterday's news. Of course I'm ready. As long as you're with me, I don't care where *there* is."

Sam and Sunni were thrilled to see us that afternoon. "Y'all sure missed a whole lotta ruckus around here. Was a good thing you decided to leave when you did," Sam said, giving me a huge hug.

"There were reporters here for days, thinking they had a story, sniffing around like hound dogs," Sunni said. "But you know the town folk. Not one of them woulda given you away. When every line they tried ended at a dead end, they all left, as quick as they came."

"Some woman stopped and left this for you. Said if you ever showed up again to be sure you got it."

My hands shook as I tried to get it open. Jack pulled a knife from his pocket, slit the envelope, and handed it back to me, all the while his eyes never leaving my face. "Who's it from?" he asked.

"Angie."

Callie ~ I suppose you're happy now. You never did understand Jason. All he ever wanted was to marry you. He's always loved you, and now he's dead. I knew he was coming to find you, try to talk some sense into you. I'll track you down myself if I ever find out you had anything to do with his death.

Jason was wrong. There's not a single thing lovable about you.

I handed Jack the note. His eyes turned hard and cold as he read it. Positioning myself to make eye contact with him, I touched his face gently.

"Hey, it doesn't matter what she says, Jack. She can't hurt me. And he can't ever hurt me again. You keep telling me that, and you've done such a good job of convincing me, I believe it to the depths of my soul. Thank you, sincerely."

He wrapped me in is arms. After a few minutes, Sam cleared his throat behind us.

"Before you kids go getting all lovey dovey again, Sunni an' me got something to tell you."

"Sam an' me is getting hitched," she blurted.

"That's wonderful!" I said, throwing my arms around Sam, then Sunni.

Even Jack seemed to be moved. He gave Sam a bear hug and kissed Sunni on the cheek. "Got any plans for a date yet?"

"Sometime soon, but nothing definite. Won't be nothing too big, just close friends."

Chapter Sixteen

ARE YOU SITTING DOWN?

*I*t was a small affair at the Amber Rose. "Seems right to have it here," Sam said. "My Rose would be real happy for Sunni an' me," he said, giving his new wife a hug. Jack and I offered to send them on a honeymoon, but they didn't want to leave until after the High Peaks Art Festival the following month. Sunni had several paintings she'd put on display, and she had others she wanted to finish.

Walking in the door a few days later, Jack kissed me senseless then asked, "What's the occasion?"

The lights were dimmed, candles lit, soft music playing. "I know how much you love it, so we're having steak and mushrooms and lots of goodies. Should be ready in a minute, but if you're going to kiss me like that, I'll turn the grill off. Dinner can wait."

"We have all night to feast on each other. Let's not let this banquet go to waste. Did I miss a birthday?"

"Well, it's an anniversary of sorts. Believe it or not, it's been nine months today since I first saw your surly face in the Amber Rose."

"I remember it like it was yesterday," he teased.

"Go wash up, cowboy, and I'll get your grub on."

"You say such sweet things, ma'am. Coming right up."

"Remember that later."

"I don't need to remember it," he said softly, "because I never forget."

Dinner was a tender and romantic affair. I couldn't have been happier.

"I have to go to Denver this weekend," I said as I lay satisfied in Jack's arms. "I have clients who sold their house last year and are finally ready to buy a new one. How silly am I that I hate the thought of being gone from you for a whole day? You're such a drug to me. Every day I wait, but it doesn't seem to go away."

Jack continued to run his fingers through my hair in that special way – twirling it as he got to the end. Over and over, soothing, drugging. I knew this was the perfect time to share my secret, knew there would never be a more tender time to tell him the news.

"Jack," I started . . .

"Angel," he said at the same moment.

We smiled at each other and he said, "There's something I need to tell you."

I touched his face and said, "Then you go first, because I have something to tell you, too."

"Ladies first," he whispered. "I've put it off this long and I'm not anxious to rush in now, so go ahead. What is it you have to say?"

"We're having a baby," I blurted. "I think it might have been the night of the big storm . . ."

His body went completely still. His fingers no longer moved through my hair. I rose on one elbow to look at his face, his familiar face that was now motionless, eyes suddenly unresponsive. "Are you upset? I know we hadn't planned it, but I didn't think you'd be displeased."

He focused on me now, sort of. "How are you feeling?" he asked. An empty question, not because he wanted to know, but because it seemed to be expected.

He unwrapped himself and stepped into his jeans. I watched his muscular body from behind, wanting to know what he was feeling.

"Where are you going?" I asked as he walked into the front room, buttoning his shirt. I scrambled out of bed and threw on my robe, putting my arms around his waist from behind. "I'm sorry, Jack, I should have prepared you better. I didn't think you'd be so shocked."

"I'm not shocked, Callie. Just thinking, that's all," he said as he continued to stare out the window. He called me Callie. Not 'little one,' not 'angel,' not 'lover' - Callie. He only called me Callie in public.

"What did you want to tell me?" I wanted him to talk to me - about anything. I wanted to touch his soul, to have him look at me and tell me it was going to be all right, that *we* were going to be all right.

"Nothing important," he responded hollowly. "You get some rest. I'll see you soon."

"Where are you going?" I asked, the desperation coming through to my own ears.

"I need to take care of some things. I need to get them done before Thursday. I'll stay at my place tonight so I can get an early start."

"Please don't leave. Let's talk this out."

"Nothing to talk out. It'll be okay. I love you, but I need time to think."

"Time to *think*?" I asked incredulously as I pulled away from him. "Time to think about *what*? Whether or not you want to be a daddy? A little late to wonder about that now! And are you kidding me that you tell me you love me but you're walking out the door because you need some time to *think*? Don't do this, Jack."

In my own ears I sounded like a fishwife. I wasn't going to beg him. *Step back, Callie, step back. Let him go.* I could feel the tears stinging my eyes. *Dammit. Don't you dare cry in front of him. He needs to get used to the idea, that's all. Let him leave.*

He touched my cheek and kissed me on the forehead, "I'll be back. I have some things I need to deal with, I'll be back soon, just give me a little time." He was gone.

Time? He loved kids. Why wasn't he thrilled? He'd make a perfect father. In my wildest dreams I wouldn't have imagined he'd react this way. I was not going to let it upset me. I had enough to deal with. I had a busy day ahead of me and needed to get some sleep. I was always so tired these days, and this had absolutely drained me.

Throughout the night I'd reach for him, needing him, wanting his arms to comfort the hurt in me. It would get through to my consciousness that he wasn't there, and the tears would gently fall until I fell back into troubled sleep. My mind refused to accept that he might go to ground again. I wasn't sure I could survive it. Not now. Not after all we'd been through. Not with the baby. Surely I was wrong.

Anger and panic and tears warred inside me. There was no way I would mention it to Marge when I arrived in Denver. We were busy all day with contractual obligations, and it was a relief I had something to occupy my time, my mind. I hadn't heard from him since he left last night. Fortunately, there was so much to do to divert me.

I'll be heading home tonight. If you're around, please, Jack, let's talk.

Getting back into Nederland, panic settled in. I alternated between praying he was waiting for me and being furious that he would leave like that. Maybe I was totally wrong, and the fire would be lit and Jack would have a meal ready.

It was dark, the house was cold. *Where are you, Jack?* I wondered as I flipped on a few lights. Everything was as it had been. The chess set sat on the dining table. I let out a sob. I went to get firewood and passed the stairs to *Callie's Eyrie*. I remembered the day I came home when he had it finished. There was not a square inch here he didn't inhabit. *Please, God, let him be coming back.*

I brought as much warmth as I could into the stillness. I fixed eggs because I had to have something to eat, not because I was hungry. If I weren't pregnant, I would've gone days without eating. I sat on the bed and opened my computer.

Dear Jack ~ You have to know what you're doing to me. It's hard to even breathe. I can't believe you walked out again. Please. There's no part of me that understands this. Even if you need time, don't you think I deserve an explanation?

I lay on the bed where we'd spent so many memorable nights and mornings. My tears made the pillow wet but I wasn't aware I was crying. I didn't know how to stop. Sleep finally won.

Dear Jack ~ I don't know where you are, but you never leave me. My thoughts are jumbled. I keep trying to make sense of it. I'm home now, but I'm not alone. You're in every part of this house. There's not one place I look and don't see you laughing, holding your arms open for me, kissing me. And somehow, I keep breathing. I'm not sure how, but I'm always surprised by it.

NEITHER SAM NOR SUNNI HAD SEEN HIM NOR HEARD FROM HIM, AND I knew both of them were concerned for me. I made it through the day - somehow. I was becoming fearful of the nights. In the middle of the night when I woke, I forgot for a minute. When I remembered, the pain was intense. My fingers flew over the keyboard.

How can I bear this?
You were a lightning bolt
Out of a clear sky
How did I get here?
I was content
But there you were
Immediately intense
So much attraction
So much affection, so many words
We shared caring, friendship, love
Embers flared
But the intensity of friendship
Outweighed it all
'We'll be friends forever, little one' – just words
I miss you so much

I'm so tired of crying
We were so far past you going to ground
You gave me love
You promised me honesty
You broke your promises
Silence – painful deafening heart-piercing silence
Where's the truth?
Where's the lie?
I want to hide, to cry
To scream, to heal
How could you?
How can you?
How can you scream so loudly into my heart
And breathe so tenderly into my soul
For so long and not care anymore?
'We'll be friends forever, little one' – just words
I miss you so much
I'm so tired of crying
Were the words not real?
How could you so easily let go?
Be gone? Be such a coward?
I thought I knew you
But where is our honesty?
Where are the words?
Don't lie – I need truth
Silence has become your lie
It's breaking me
Where is our core? Our friendship? Our caring?
At every corner I search for my best friend
His shoulder to ease my pain
Friends don't stab fatally
Without caring, do they?
'We'll be friends forever, little one' – just words
I miss you so much
I'm so tired of crying

The sun was shining when I woke. I had rested. I was fine for a while. For a time I was able to do things around the house, fix a meal, clean the kitchen. But how do you shut off your brain?

Dear Jack ~ I know it's not your intention to destroy me, and I won't let you. It's the silence I hate the most. How do you deal with something when you don't know what it is? I keep believing this isn't who you are, but how do I know what to believe any more?

IT WASN'T EVEN NOON YET, BUT I WAS TIRED OF BEING AWAKE. I crawled under the covers and fell asleep, welcome, blissful sleep.

By the afternoon I knew I couldn't stay where I was. I didn't want to leave the house, so maybe I could go to *Callie's Eyrie* and take pictures. Rounding the last turn on the staircase, I remembered seeing Jack there, knowing life was complete, believing I'd always be as happy as I was in that moment. What a fool. I headed back to the living room.

When I saw the chess set on the table, I had a notion to throw it piece by piece into the fire, destroying it as I was being destroyed, but I couldn't. When I picked up the first piece I knew I could never damage something so lifelike. I cried as I ran my thumb over the Queen's carved robe, thinking of the heart that made it, conceived it. I gently reset the pieces one by one. Even the workmanship of the box was clever, and I could see clearly the joy of playing chess with Jack.

I rushed through the task, wanting them out of sight. I thought about the Amber Rose but didn't want to face anyone with my battling emotions, puffy face, heartache. I settled on a book I found on the shelf. It was a bestseller, surely it would occupy time.

But I couldn't see the words, just kept reliving the last time he was here. I needed sleep, but every time I closed my eyes, I saw him - in the bed next to me, in the kitchen, with Sam. I couldn't drink alcohol because of the baby, but I craved the sweet oblivion. Amazingly, I slept until morning.

Jack was too much a part of this place, I knew I couldn't stay. After hours of virtually not moving, I called Marge. I knew what street Jack lived on but didn't know the exact address. I'd ask Marge to find it for me. I didn't know what I'd do with the information and didn't think he was there, but I needed to know.

I chided myself that I was feeling like a stalker, and I could feel that desperation, that insanity of needing to know where he was. Was he hurting like I was? Was he with someone else? How could he walk away, no contact? I didn't know what to think, only that I needed an explanation, a chance to talk it out.

When she called back, I knew it didn't bode well when her first words were, "Are you sitting down?"

"What is it, Marge? Tell me, dammit."

Marge had been as gentle as possible, but there hadn't been any way to cushion the blow. "Oh, honey, he owns that house - and several others - with his wife. And, Callie, there's more . . ."

Chapter Seventeen

GOING HOME

$\mathcal{T}$he phone fell to the floor as the numbness permeated my body. I could hear Marge talking but I didn't care, didn't want to hear more. It didn't matter, nothing mattered. My greatest fear was what was going to happen when the numbness wore off.

Was it possible to feel nothing, absolutely nothing? I put on my coat and stepped outside. The snow was starting and the ground looked like fairy dust. I didn't care. I didn't notice when my hands started to freeze, or when people called to me to hurry home, or offered me a ride, or asked if I was okay. I put one foot in front of the other.

Jack has a wife, I'm going to have his baby. Jack has a wife, I'm going to have his baby. It was all I could grasp. I continued on mindlessly, not wanting to think anymore, certainly not wanting to feel. Somewhere along the way I became mindful I was the one who would be there for our baby, no *my* baby.

The thought brought me up short. The sun was setting and the snow was falling hard. It was eerily quiet and I didn't have a clue where I was. There was another life I had to take care of now. I had to pull my scattered attention together no matter how sorry I was feeling for myself.

I retraced my footprints in the snow, hoping to catch their trail to a familiar path before the snow covered them completely. The cold in my hands and feet was unbearable. I slipped once, cut my hand on a jutting rock. I had to get home, had to get in out of this cold.

Cresting the hill, I saw the lights and smoke from the chimneys below. I knew where I was and hurried to get inside, to get warm. Maybe Jack would be waiting for me. *No!* He was gone. He'd never be waiting again. How was I going to make it? How could he have lied to me so completely? How could Sam and my father have let it happen? There's no way they couldn't have known. Was I actually that blind? Was I blind because I'd *wanted* to be?

Cold, numb, and bruised, the sanctuary of my bath was my focus, purposefully avoiding noticing my surroundings. There wasn't an inch of this place that wasn't saturated with Jack. I wouldn't think about that now, I had to get warm. I struggled to remove my boots with frozen hands. I was in slow motion as I removed my clothes. Finally, blessedly, I slipped under the balmy water.

The sobs drowned out the sound of the running water. I was warm but not yet numb. I thought of the first morning when Jack walked into the room while I was in the tub. Please, no, I didn't want to remember. I wanted oblivion. I woke up in my bed. I don't recall how or when I got there.

The phone was ringing, but it didn't matter. I didn't want anyone intruding on my space. I stayed under the covers and watched the snowfall, turned the ringer off, and slept more. The sun was setting the next time my eyes opened. It was probably the growling in my stomach that woke me. I had to eat.

The pounding wouldn't stop. What *was* that noise? Please, go away. It continued. I threw the covers off and opened the door. Sam was wagging his finger at me.

"You been holed up here long enough. Why ain't you answering your phone? Your pa is worried sick about you. Good God almighty, young 'un. What's the matter with you? You sick? You look like hell."

"Nothing, Sam. Please, just leave me in peace."

"When was the last time you had a decent meal?"

"I have no idea. Thank you for checking on me. I'm fine, now go."

"I'll be back in twenty minutes. If you lock this door I'm gonna pound it down. You gonna eat if I have to spoon feed you like a baby."

True to his word, he came back with a plate piled high. The thought of it made me nauseated, but Sam insisted I have some. When I'd eaten all I could, he packed the rest and put it in the refrigerator.

"You get hungry, you pull that out. It'll be good for the next few days."

"Thank you. Now please leave me alone."

"You know I can be here in two minutes flat. All you gotta do is ask."

"Why didn't you tell me Jack was married?"

"*What?* Who told you that?" He shut the door and came back into the room.

"My secretary found out that Jack's house here, and his other houses all over the state, are owned by him and his wife. Why didn't you and Daddy ever tell me? You knew how close Jack and I were."

"You got it all wrong, sweet child."

"Go, Sam. I can't take any more right now." I closed and locked the door behind him.

Two hours later, the pounding started again.

"Sweet Jesus, can't you people leave me alone?" I shouted as I opened the door. My father pushed right past me into the living room. "Sam's right, you *do* look like hell."

"Sam needs to mind his own business."

"Sam's concerned about you, and rightly so. You got it all wrong. We need to talk."

I headed to the kitchen to get some food, suddenly hungry. "Have you eaten yet?" I asked. "Sam brought food earlier. I'll fix it for both of us. But before you explain why everyone chose to lie to me, let me tell *you* something. I'm pregnant. Yes, Daddy, I'm going to have Jack Franklin's baby. *Now* how do you feel about not telling me about his *wife*?" Yes, that shrieking was coming from my mouth, and not one part of me cared.

"And as soon as he found out about the baby, he left. Poof, like smoke. No contact, no communication whatsoever. Gone. The high and mighty Jack Franklin that everyone loves and adores. The man who can do no wrong." Breaking down in fitful sobs, I said, "I'm not sure I can survive this."

He took me in his arms and led me to the couch. "Someone should have told you. I'm so sorry."

My cries grew even louder. "Someone should have *told me*? How could you not have?"

"It's not at all what you think, pun'kin. Any one of us would have told you. I guess we all thought the other would. God knows I told him enough times he had to be honest with you."

"Well, he wasn't."

"Let me explain."

I laid down on the edge of the couch and put my feet in his lap. After he put a blanket over me, his words were quiet, painful. My father sat absently patting his little girl, telling me in different ways that his heart broke for Jack's and my pain.

"What? Under the circumstances, how could you have any sympathy for someone who could do this to me?"

"You don't understand. Jack has been through trauma like few others I've known. You have to give him a little more time to come to grips with your situation."

Throwing my legs off of the couch, I sat up, angry. "Are you *serious*? Jack needs *my* understanding? Are you *kidding me*?" My voice rose. My hands shook. I wanted to throw something, anything.

"Listen to me, Callie, just listen. Jack *was* married. He was married to a beautiful woman named Marcie. They were very much in love. When Marcie was eight months pregnant with their son, a drunk driver ran a red light and hit her broadside. She wasn't wearing a seat belt, and she was hit on the driver's side.

"The baby died instantly. Marcie lived several more days after that. Jack has been up here ever since. Someone should have told you, but I always thought Jack would, and I didn't want to interfere. It should make you feel better knowing Jack isn't married. He hasn't been leading a double life. He probably can't bring himself to talk about it. It's only been a few years."

I was completely still, quiet. "Callie? What is it, honey?"

How many times could my world be rocked by revelations and I maintain my sanity?

"Nothing. Thank you for telling me. I'm very tired now. I'm going to bed. Thank you for coming up. The bed in the guest room is made. Make yourself at home."

I wanted to make it to my room before I broke down. Without turning back, I said, "I don't mean to sound ungrateful or inhospitable. It's your house, after all, so please, make yourself at home."

What he couldn't possibly have understood was the intensified heartache this information brought. How could I ever compete with the ghost of a dead woman? A *perfect* dead woman. I'd struggle now with the thought that, in my whole life, even if Jack were to come back, I could never replace the woman that had been so cruelly taken from him, the mother of his unborn son, the one that time would make larger-than-life. How do you measure up to something like that? How do you help someone heal from that kind of heartbreak?

"Listen," my father said, putting his hand on my shoulder. "Why don't you think about coming back to town for a while? I hate you being here by yourself, hours away. At least until you get things figured out and know what you want to do."

"I'll give it some thought, I promise."

"I'm not going to stay unless you need me. I thought you should know before any more days went by. I didn't trust Sam to tell you the whole truth. I had no idea Jack wouldn't have told you before now."

"I'll be fine. Thank you for coming up here to deliver the news personally."

He pulled me into his arms and held me. I kept telling myself I needed to wait until he left before I broke down. I could hold off a minute or two.

"Now might be a good time to think about building that house you've always wanted. You have a baby on the way. Perfect time to think about getting a fresh start on your life."

"It makes a lot of sense. And I promise I'll come to town in the next few days. I know in my heart of hearts I can't stay here much longer."

"That's my girl. It will all work itself out."

Watching him pull out of the driveway, instead of wanting to go to bed, I now wanted so much to talk to Jack.

DEAR JACK ~ WHEN YOU LEFT, MY DRUGS OF CHOICE WERE TRAGIC songs and tears - trying to erase you from my mind, trying to erase us from my memory. I'd walk in the door and see you. You filled my world, everything I knew included you. I kept reading your letter, never wanting to believe it was a lie. Why couldn't you have told me? How could you turn it off like that?

I've stayed in the Fortress of Solitude *because leaving would mean leaving you behind. Now I know I have to. I can't replace what you've lost, and I can't stay with what I've lost.*

Daddy came up tonight. I told him about the baby. I told him I found out you were married. I hadn't told him before how special our relationship was, but I'm sure he must've known when you built Callie's Eyrie. *I poured my heart out to him about how much I missed my friend and how broken I've been. It was a memorable bonding time.*

He told me about Marcie. Oh, Jack, I'm sorry. I know I can't heal that pain, but I'm sorry for your loss. I'm having a hard time forgiving you for not telling me yourself, but obviously my lack of forgiveness will have no impact on you.

When we met, my psyche absorbed you. I believed what we shared was unique, and while we were wildly attracted to each other, it wasn't just sex. I'm a sensual creature, but something about what we shared took it to a different level.

I was so happy with our friendship, my body always so aware, my mind enhanced. I was so wounded when you left. How could I not take it personally, as a rejection of me? How could this happen from the man with whom I'd shared such depths of friendship and heights of passion? I questioned my discernment. How could I have been so wrong?

For a while, heartrending, gut-wrenching songs drowned out your voice, your words, your desire, your being that existed in my being. Your leaving made no sense. I was heartbroken because what you and I have is addicting, and you walked away. When I found out you were married, I was in a tailspin. How would I ever trust anyone again?

I'm not sure which was more shocking, that you were married, or that there actually was someone else, the tragically deceased wife. All of it would've been so much easier to understand if it had come directly from you. Can you comprehend that the Jack I knew so well would not be capable of slamming the door like that? Have you even considered what your cowardice might do to me?

Daddy's visit helped. I'm leaving here soon. I'll always wish it had been you who'd told me. I'll probably never understand that part of it, but I can get on with my life now.

I'm writing this more for me than you. It's my closure. You won't hear from me again, no matter how difficult my days or nights might be. You have what you want. You are now unencumbered. I fear I'll always love you, but like Jason, I won't allow you or anyone else to destroy me. I'm in charge of my life. You no longer get to steal my joy. Big words, but I'll get there.

I HAD PURPOSE AGAIN. I SPENT MOST OF THE NIGHT CLEANING AND

packing. I was going to stay in Daddy's cottage. I'd build the house of my dreams, and I was going to heal, although right now I wasn't sure how. I had something to live for. It still hurt to breathe, but I'd gone hours without crying. I packed the car and made a final sweep to make sure everything was in order.

The phone rang as I locked the door. My heart raced when I saw it was Jack. I'd waited for this, it was all I had wanted - to hear his voice, to make everything okay, to right my world.

I didn't answer. He left a long message. I erased it without listening. If I was going to start over, I didn't need to hear excuses and explanations about his perfect wife. I had turned a corner. I was going to make it.

I stopped at the Amber Rose. One look at me and Sam knew what was happening. Tears pooled in his eyes as he held his arms open. We rocked in each other's arms.

"This is déjà vu. I lost your ma and pa just like this."

"You will *never* lose me, Sam, never. I have to get some things worked out. I'll be up here often. You think I don't want my baby to know you? I'd never do to you what my parents did, you have my word. You're a part of me, and a part of us."

"I'll come hunt you down if you become a stranger."

"We'll be back often, but you can't make me cry right now. I'm hanging by a thread. I've gone a few hours without crying, but I'm afraid of what will happen if I start again. Always know I love you. I'll be back within the month."

"We'll keep an eye on the place 'til you get back. It'll be ready for you."

"What would I have done without you? And you and Sunni are going to be part of my pregnancy and my baby's childhood. You won't get rid of me that easily."

Driving away I started to cry, but knew I wouldn't stop if I didn't get it under control. It was time to make arrangements.

"DADDY, I TOOK OUR CONVERSATION TO HEART. I'M COMING HOME."

"*Now?*" There was panic in his voice.

"Don't worry, I'll stay in the cottage for a while. That is, of course, if you don't mind. If you do, I'll find a place to rent until I can get a house built. That shouldn't be a problem."

"No problem at all, I was just surprised, that's all. I'll make sure everything is ready when you get here. When will that be?"

"In less than two hours."

"You've already left? How did you do that so quickly?" It did sound like panic in his voice.

"After you left last night, I thought about our conversation. I couldn't bear to be there without Jack, and since he's not coming back, I need to get on with my life. Is something wrong?"

"No, no, not at all. I'll have to get things together in a hurry."

"Please don't bother. I'm very capable of getting sheets changed and the place aired out all on my own. It'll give me something to do. You wouldn't have known it last night, but I'm a big girl now."

I tried to inject humor. "But you have to promise me something. No talk about Jack, okay? It's too raw, too painful. There may come a time when I can think about him, but not now. I need to not cry so I can heal. Deal?"

"If you say so, but I'm not sure that's a good idea. I know he had to have loved you."

"No! We're not going there. Please, Daddy, I need it to be this way for now."

"Whatever you say. I'll leave the timing to you."

MY DAD OPENED THE DOOR BEFORE I EVEN GOT TO THE FRONT PORCH.

"Well, you look a whole lot better than you did last night. Quite a dramatic change."

"Thank you, you helped a lot. If I don't think about it, time will heal me. If I think about it, I'll fall apart, and I can't afford that. I have to make a new life for us. I'll never trust another man again, but I have a baby to think about now. Please help me."

"Honey, you and I need to talk."

"Not if it's about Jack."

"No, no, I, too, have been keeping a secret. Not for any reason other than I know what you've been going through the past few months, and I didn't mean to *not* tell you."

"Is it going to rock my world, Father?"

"Father - so pedantic. I don't want it to rock your world, but that will be up to you."

"Spill it. Now." I was preparing myself, steeling myself for what he would tell me about Jack.

"I've met someone."

It took me a minute to understand what he was saying. "What?"

"I don't want you to be upset."

I started laughing. I kept laughing until I was sure I'd lost my mind.

"What it is, Callie?"

"Why did you think that would upset me? I'm so happy for you!" I said, throwing my arms around him. "When do I get to meet her? Genuinely, if you're happy, I'm happy."

"That's why I was concerned about you coming here so quickly. She stays here most days, or rather, most nights. I didn't know if you'd think it was too soon after your mom."

"You spent years taking care of Mom when she was sick. You deserve to be happy. Where is she? And what's her name?"

"I sent her to the store until I had a chance to tell you. I wasn't sure you wouldn't be upset. And her name is Della. We're pretty crazy about each other."

"Well, call her and tell her to come home. I have absolutely no problem with it."

"Well, good then, because now I have some exciting news for you. You know I have a pretty close relationship with Montgomery? I called him after I found out you were coming home, didn't divulge too much information but told him you wanted to build a house and asked him for a favor because you needed something to occupy your time right now. He's years out for new clients and is just getting ready to leave town, but he told me he'd fit you in first thing in the morning if you can work that out, being as how he and I go way back."

"Are you kidding? Please tell me you're serious! Montgomery? *The* Montgomery?"

"Yep, 8:30, his office. I told him you're one of his biggest fans. He was happy to rearrange his schedule."

"Oh, Daddy, *thank you*! It'll give me something to concentrate on. It'll be exactly what I need to take my mind off of the mess I've made of the rest of my life. In the meantime, I'm going to unpack. You sure you don't mind me staying in the cottage for a while? Seriously, I can get a rental or go stay with Marge."

"Wouldn't hear of it. It'll be nice. You can get to know Della, we can share in the excitement of building your house, we can be here for you during your pregnancy. It'll be great, you'll see."

"You've been a lifeline to me so many times."

"It's what fathers are for."

Chapter Eighteen

EMPTY HOUSE

The next morning was so different than the past few weeks. I woke with excitement about my upcoming meeting with Montgomery. I knew exactly what I wanted my house to look like, had envisioned it for years since I first saw his work.

My mind kept sliding to Jack. My heart would start its yearning cry. It was only the thought of having a new project that kept me sane. I wanted him. I couldn't have him. *Move on, Callie, move on.*

I arrived early. My mental image of Montgomery was as an elderly, scholarly sort with a neat beard. Maybe he even smoked a pipe. His secretary was older and pleasant. She made me miss Marge. I suppose my hiatus would end sooner than expected. I wondered if I'd ever be able to go back to the cabin and stay. *Give it time, Callie, one day at a time.*

"Good morning, Ms. Weston. May I get you some coffee?"

"No, thank you, I'm good." I couldn't believe how nervous I was. Not only was I going to meet Montgomery, but he was going to build me a house. It was a dream come true.

"Mr. Montgomery will see you now. Follow me, please."

The office was classic Montgomery. His signature was everywhere. We walked to the end of a wide hallway. She knocked on the door, waited momentarily, and then said, "You may go in now."

I could hardly contain my excitement. The office was spectacular - and empty. The door closed behind me . . .

"*You!* What are *you* doing here?"

He leaned against the door, arms folded, blocking my way.

I lifted my chin and felt the heat rising in my face. "Let me pass. I don't know what kind of a sick joke this is, but let me out of here."

"Not until you listen to me, little one. Please hear me out."

"First off, don't call me that. You no longer have the right. You made your decision." Blood was pounding in my head, rushing in audible waves. I wanted to slap him, shriek at him, pummel his chest. I took a calming breath.

"Secondly, what you want is now irrelevant because it's too late. You had plenty of time to explain, you chose not to. I don't care to hear it. I'm getting on with my life."

"Everything you've said is true. I've been an idiot. I wouldn't give me the time of day, but you've always been so much smarter than I. Please, five minutes, that's all I ask. If you still want to leave, I'll figure out a way to let you walk out of here."

He touched my hair. "I've missed you so much."

"Don't you dare." Tears threatened. I didn't want to cry. "Get out of my way, Jack."

"I can't. I need to explain, please."

"*You* need? Is that what matters here, what *you* need? You should have thought of that last week when it would've mattered. And where is John Montgomery?" I felt duped. Had my father been in on this?

He took a step toward me, I took a step back. "Don't. I'm hanging by a thread. If you care about me at all, you'll let me go, for me, for our baby. I can't cry anymore."

A winsome smile crossed his face, a face that would forever haunt me. "I've always loved your honesty. Please, will you sit? Give me a few minutes? Hear me out? Allow me to finally be honest with you like I should have been a long time ago?"

Could I have full closure to put him behind me without hearing what he'd never told me? Was I fooling myself because just looking at him was a balm to my soul? Would I always wonder what had driven him away? Did I care?

Of course I cared. I collapsed on the oversized leather chair because I feared falling down. I couldn't put it all together.

"Do you want some water?"

"Yes, please."

His fingers touched mine as he handed me a glass. I pulled away as though burned. "You're stunning. Whether you believe me or not, you haven't left my side since I walked out."

"Stop it. Why are you here?"

"Open your eyes. Look around. You're in the office of John Montgomery."

"And?"

Crouching next to the chair, he was eye level with me when he said, "Callie, I *am* John Montgomery."

It took a moment for his words to register. "Wait a minute. How can that be? Then who's Jack Franklin?"

Without breaking eye contact, he made a slight bow of his head and said, "At your service, ma'am. John Franklin Montgomery, known to my closest friends as Jack."

The rabbit hole was swallowing me. "None of this makes sense."

"Will you stay, hear what I have to say, and then you can make your decision with the information you should have had months ago?"

When I didn't respond, he began, "I know I've left it way too long, but every time I tried to tell you, I couldn't seem to find the right words. So many times I wanted to tell you I'd build you anything you wanted, anywhere you wanted. Then you'd wax poetic about John Montgomery and I'd think it might be better said at a later time. Time and again I wanted to tell you about Marcie, but the truth is, I was scared."

I sat silently, reality slipping further away. Jack sat in the chair next to me. He took my fidgeting hand as my mind raced through possibilities. This was an unreal turn of events I couldn't seem to wrap my brain around.

"When I'd think I could tell you about Marcie, I was so afraid of that dark side of me, and it was easier to let it slide. For that I'm truly sorry."

Tears warmed my cheeks. "I know how much you must have loved her, and I understand it would be hard to replace that." Jack handed me a handkerchief.

"Again, things are not always as they seem."

"I can never compete with a dead woman, Jack."

"Trust me, there is no competition." His thumb wiped an errant tear. He touched the end of my hair and wrapped it around his finger. He soothed me and whispered unintelligible words, kind and patient and tender sounds that made me all the more heartsick, all the more tearful.

"I take full responsibility for not telling you before. It is not a pretty story. After I tell you *my* truth, you can decide whether or not you'll ever be able to love me again."

"That'll be a tough decision. It's not a switch. I don't get to flip it on and off at will." I wished I could turn off the tears, but they ran at their own discretion down my cheeks.

"As long as I live, I'll spend every remaining day of my life showing you how much I love you if you'll let me." My breathing slowed. He knew he had my attention.

"There's only one other person alive who knows what I'm going to tell you, and he only knows part of it. He'll never repeat it to another living soul, and I'll never do anything to change people's perception of what happened. People believe what they want to believe, they see what they want to see." With a gentle sweep of his hand to encompass the room, he said, "Case in point." I blushed.

"It was all a sham," he began. "When I first married her, I did love Marcie – as much as you can love someone you don't really know. We weren't married long before I understood that Marcie was the only person in the world that Marcie cared about.

"I could give her the lifestyle she craved. She never understood I never wanted any of it. I went to the auctions, the balls, the soirees, the premiers, all because of her. She craved high society, money, prestige, the social position. At first I was in love so I indulged her. By the time she told me she was pregnant, I had no feelings left for her, but I knew I'd do whatever was necessary for my child to have a balanced life, but Marcie wouldn't quit drinking."

Jack wasn't looking at me anymore. He was back in his own hell, a place only he could see. I rubbed his hand soothingly.

"One night when she was eight months pregnant, I came home to find her drunk again. I told her she wasn't fit to be a mother. I told her I'd give her enough money so she could live in luxury if she'd relinquish her rights to our son. I had hired nurses and guards for months to make sure she wouldn't drink, but she always found a way.

"She laughed at me and told me, not for the first time, that she'd never wanted to be a mother, that she couldn't wait to get this brat out of her. Then she called me a fool. Told me she couldn't believe how naive I was, that the baby wasn't even mine. She'd been having an affair with Clark since before we got married."

I gasped.

"I apologize for that night. I hadn't seen Clark since Marcie's death, and I couldn't find anything in me to be civil, to forgive him. The night we saw him, you had become my world. I'd done such a good job of burying the past, and then there he was and it was all new and raw again. I let myself believe it was some kind of a sign, that I'd never get out from under their shadow, that even in death she'd destroy me.

"But even more so than Marcie, I'd been devastated by Clark. He'd been my best friend and business partner for ten years. I understood her black heart, but felt like I'd been truly betrayed by him.

"Anyway, I didn't want her to know how shocked I was as her words sank in. 'Then go to him,' I told her. 'Let him raise your son.'

"She said she'd never give me a divorce, that every time I saw the baby I'd be reminded she was sleeping with my best friend. I've never hated anyone more than I did Marcie in that moment. She was evil, and I grieved for the child she carried. As God is my witness, all I wanted to do was hit her.

"If you and I are to have total honesty between us, you have to understand the darkness I was in. She was out of control and threw priceless items she'd been so busy collecting over the previous year. I imagined the satisfaction of strangling the life out of her.

"I actually wondered if I would have struck her if she hadn't been pregnant. When I became conscious of where my mind was going, I knew I had allowed her venom to poison me. I walked up the stairs to the room we'd shared. The whole time she was yelling, calling me weak, telling me I was a coward because I wouldn't fight with her."

I remained silent, barely breathing, not moving, listening to his heartbreak, the broken lives pouring out around me.

"I was so disgusted with her, with me. When I got to our room, I was totally composed, wondering how I hadn't seen it. Where had we gone wrong, and how had we gotten to this point? I grieved for the son I'd just lost that had never been mine. I wondered how to disentangle myself from the nightmare that had become my life.

"Standing at the window, watching the rain fall steadily in a pitch black night, I saw her drive away. I hoped she was going to Clark and that she'd never come back. Then I remembered how drunk she was, certainly in no condition to drive. I thought about calling Clark, but there weren't any civil words I could say to him. What could he have done at that point anyway?

"The irony of what happened was that it was someone else who ran the red light. A drunk driver slammed into Marcie's car. He hit the driver's side, and it took almost two hours to get her out. The baby was dead, and Marcie was in a coma. Before they even got her out of the car, the police were at my door.

"Marcie lived for two days, never regaining consciousness. I stayed by her side the whole time, overwhelmed with guilt that I didn't care if she lived. People thought I was the grieving husband. Because the accident wasn't her fault, they never checked her blood alcohol levels. They didn't do an autopsy. They never knew she was drunk.

"There was a whole bubble of myth that had begun to grow before I even knew about the crash. I became the grieving widower who had lost his family. I was the tragic Heathcliff that every woman wanted to soothe. But I couldn't talk to anyone. There was no part of me that was a good enough actor to feign that I cared she was gone.

"When I cried, it was for the innocent child who knew nothing of life before he lost it, and for Clark's betrayal. Clark never once showed up at the hospital or the funeral. I wanted him to hurt, if not for Marcie, then for the son he lost or the friend he'd betrayed. I was having a hard time dealing with my anger, dealing with my guilt.

"I went to Nederland. I threw myself into finishing the home I'd always wanted, the one Marcie wouldn't even take the time to come see. She wanted mansions, society. She couldn't stand the thought of being in the middle of nowhere for even a weekend. I used my middle name, and those close to me have always called me Jack. I hid. Even more of a mystery grew around the tragic life of John Montgomery, the renowned architect who had mysteriously disappeared after the horrific death of his beautiful young wife and son.

"If I'd taken you to see my house, you would have known immediately. I didn't mind telling you about me, but I was never sure how to be honest about Marcie. I was never sure how to get past the blame I carry about her."

He was absently rubbing my knee. I knelt between his legs, putting my head on his chest. My heart was breaking for this man who had such an amazing capacity to love.

"You didn't kill her. She made her choices. I'm sorry for all of it, but you didn't do it."

"When you told me you were pregnant, the guilt overwhelmed

me. I'd spent so many months planning for my child, only to find out I never had one. I knew you weren't Marcie, but all the lines blurred. When I left you, I went to a little place I have in Telluride. I didn't ever want to go through what I'd been through again. I convinced myself I didn't deserve you and what you were offering. I was covered in so much anger, so much guilt for the fact I'd never once been unhappy she was dead.

"After I was done feeling sorry for myself, I knew how stupid I'd been. You're tough, but the gentlest spirit I've ever known. You appreciate everything. I was so wrapped up in my own torment I couldn't see past it, and so self-absorbed I couldn't see what I was doing to you. I finally came to grips with how selfish I was, putting you through what you must have been suffering. I had no computer with me and had shut off my phone for days. When I finally read your emails and understood you thought I was married, I couldn't even conceive of your pain.

"I knew your heart would've thought I was grieving for her, and nothing could've been further from the truth. I was being childish, feeling sorry for myself, but there's no way you could have known. I didn't blame you for not taking my call. And Marcie's name on title to all the houses was an oversight, one I have since taken care of. I called your dad and asked him not to tell you who I was because I was so afraid you wouldn't see me, that you were done with me."

This dreamlike turn of events was far from how I thought I was going to spend my morning.

"I couldn't find anything to fill the void that was my life without you in it," he said. "You aren't Marcie and there's nothing in you that would even *understand* a woman like her. I'm a fool who wants to spend the rest of his life making it up to you."

I didn't care if I was getting his shirt wet. I wrapped my arms around him and tried to grasp what I was hearing, tried to let go of my own pain.

"There were days when I thought I wouldn't be able to survive for the loss of you," I said. "There wasn't a minute that passed when you weren't with me. When you left, most of me went with you. What made it so much worse was the not knowing. You can't find answers when you don't know what the questions are. I'd told you before, you can't play the game if you're dealing with a short deck.

"Then I'd remember the baby and knew I'd do whatever needed to be done. I didn't know the heart could be torn out of the chest and keep beating. There's not a part of you I don't love – the good and the bad – the gentle and the hard. But there's no denying you crushed me."

"Oh, Callie, no one knows better than I what a jerk I've been."

"Oh no, I have a pretty good idea."

He cupped my face. "You're every fantasy I never knew I had. There's nothing in my life I want if you're not in it. I know it's not what you thought you were getting when you walked in here. You can have a house *and* me if you'll marry me. I promise we'll work through any bumps in the road together."

"Did my dad know about this?"

"I gave him fair warning that you might not be coming back today. Made sure he wouldn't press kidnapping charges if it took a while to woo you," he laughed. "But he said whatever happened, I had his blessing as long as you're happy."

"I don't know how I'd live through it if you ever left again. There'd be no turning back."

"It solved nothing, obviously, and caused only heartache for both of us. You have my solemn promise. Besides, you know about every shade of my darkness now. There are no more secrets."

"I can't live if I'm waiting for you to be gone if there's a crisis."

"If nothing else, you'll own all my houses. You can track me down," he teased. His voice gentled, his expression became serious. "But it won't ever happen. You have me from here to eternity if you're willing to give me one more chance."

"I don't have much choice, Jack," I said. "I don't want to live trying to remember how to put one foot in front of the other because you're not there."

He tilted my head and kissed me in his breathtaking way, then walked over to his desk and opened a drawer, withdrawing a small box. When he was in front of me again, the velvet lid of the box opened silently, revealing an incredible ring that had an absolute Montgomery line and feel to it.

"Did you . . ."

"Yeah. I designed it a while back. I've had it for months. The night you told me you were pregnant, I had it with me. I was going to tell you about Marcie and see if you'd still want me. When you told me we were going to have a baby, how could I possibly tell you I'd wanted to do physical harm to my dead, pregnant wife? And then I almost lost you over her ghost. I was such a fool."

He held me with strength and tenderness for what seemed like minutes. When he stepped back, he touched my face, running his thumb across my cheek. "Callie Weston, will you do me the honor of being my wife? Of loving me through good times and bad as I promise to love you? Of allowing me to be the best father to our child I can possibly be? I love you and want to spend my life showing you how much."

"I believe you love me, Jack. I don't think it was ever your intention to hurt me, but the pain of your leaving was so much worse than any physical pain Jason inflicted. I'm willing to bet forever on us, from this day forward, if you promise me only absolute honesty. That's my demand."

"There won't be a day in your life you'll regret your decision, I give you my word."

I held out my left hand so he could slip his ring on my finger. "Yes, please, I want to be your wife."

The design touched the same emotional chord in me that his houses did. I threw myself into his arms. "Oh, God, Jack. I love you so much." The tears resumed their determined course. "As long as we live, there may be three or four or more of us, but you and I will be one."

He buried his face in my neck. "Thank you."

He pushed a panel on the bookshelf. It opened to what was obviously a private entrance. He offered me his hand.

"I came here this morning to build an empty house because it's what I needed to help me survive without you. But it's not the structure that matters, it's whether or not we're there together."

"So I have an idea," he said.

"I'm listening." I snuggled against him.

"How about we get married this weekend in a quiet ceremony with only our closest family and friends, then take the next month or so traveling around the state looking at your new homes? We'll make it our honeymoon tour, making love in a half dozen John Montgomery houses. If you don't find something in the lot of them that's everything you want and more, then you name the location and tell me what you want, and I'll build it," he smiled.

My laughter erupted from the depths of my core. "Can you even imagine?" I felt almost drunk. "I not only get Jack Franklin, I get to own multiple Montgomery houses as well. Dear Lord, please don't wake me if this is a dream."

He pressed the button on the intercom, all the while keeping me close.

"Yes, Mr. Montgomery."

"Ms. Hays, I'm leaving now. I'll be in touch in the next few days."

"Of course, Mr. Montgomery."

His loving smile said it all. "Ready?"

"Beyond a shadow of a doubt."

EPILOGUE

"*A*m I waddling?" I plopped myself on the couch and put my swollen feet on the arm. Jack lifted them and set them in his lap, rubbing my tired, aching legs in gentle, circular motions.

"You've been overdoing it since we got back. You need to take it easy."

After an intimate wedding with only my father, Della, Marge, Sam, and Sunni in attendance, we'd spent at least a week at each of Jack's Colorado residences. A cabin in Telluride, a ski lodge in Aspen, a mansion in an exclusive area of Denver, a rustic hideaway in Creede, and the most perfect place on earth, his home high on the hill overlooking Barker Reservoir.

The last month or so had been a sensory overload between my passionate husband and dynamic and unusual architecture, all with Jack's flair, all with a unique personality, each a place I could easily call home. But we'd agreed our current life would be split between "the big house" in Denver and the majestic "cabin" in Nederland until after the baby was born.

"I feel like I haven't been much use at all lately," I said as my smile hid what felt suspiciously like a whine.

"In addition to keeping up with your full-time job, being a full-time lover, a full-time decorator, taking care of yourself so you're taking care of our baby, what else did you have in mind to slip into your lax schedule?"

The tears must have given me away because he pulled me onto his lap and into his arms and said, "Hey, lady, you know I'm kidding. What's going on?" His kisses were tender on my forehead but the tears started to fall anyway.

"I'm just so emotional today. I already waddle when I walk and I'm only six months pregnant and I have a long way to go and I'm going to be twice as big and I'll have a hard time getting through the door and I had to take a break when I tried to walk down to the Amber Rose earlier and what if I am still huge after she's born and what if we don't make it to the hospital in time and what if I'm not a good mom and how are you possibly going to still love me after I deliver a baby? And I hate to cry!" I finished my outpouring on a sob.

He held me. I was proud of him for not laughing out loud. He did a great job of being silent, even though his body was shaking. Taking a deep breath, he said, with a straight face, "You're going to get a lot bigger before this is done, and when you do? Guess what? I'm still going to love you, even more than I do now, if that's possible."

He smoothed strands of hair from my face. "If you have a hard time getting through the door, I'll walk behind you so I can push." I buried my face in his neck and laughed.

"We'll stay somewhere near the hospital when the time comes if that's genuinely a concern," he continued. "But we're within a half hour of where you're supposed to deliver, so if we don't make it for your first baby, more power to you. I'll be prepared." I nodded my head against him.

"And I will take you to task if I ever hear a hint of you even thinking again you might not be a good mother. Are you kidding me? Could there be anyone better? You are a caregiver by nature. You love as deeply and intensely as anyone I've known in my life. What makes you think that won't extend to the child you bring into the world? Make that the very last time the thought enters your mind."

My arms were still around his neck but I pulled back to look him in the eyes. "You're the one that's so good at loving. You've taken my hormone-driven hysteria and made me feel almost normal again."

"And by the way, if you ever get to be the size of a barn, we'll walk to the Amber Rose every day to help get you back in shape. Not because I won't still love you for all you're worth, and your girth, but you'll be miserable and hate yourself because you won't be able to pick up our daughter, so we'll work on it."

After the tears and subsequent laughter, he asked softly, "Have you thought about what you want to name her?"

I nodded. "How about you?"

He ran his fingers through my hair. "I thought we might name her Charlotte, kill two birds with one stone and name her after your mother *and* your father."

"You're so good to me," I whispered. "What would you think of Rose as a middle name? I think that would honor Sam and his Rose, and it would be a beautiful name."

"Unless you think of something better in the meantime, Charlotte Rose she is."

We sat for a long time, each lost in thought. "Did I tell you that Madeline died?" I asked. "The lady that owned the big Victorian up by the cemetery? I didn't know her but she was a friend of my dad's. I heard from her niece this morning. She inherited the house and is coming out soon to take a look at the place."

"I hope she's prepared for what she's going to find. I don't think anyone's lived there for at least thirty years."

"She's coming out to see if she wants to keep it or sell it. I told her I'd meet her when she comes to town and give her the pros and cons of both alternatives."

"Did you tell her there's not even electricity?"

"No. She's getting married in a few weeks and they're going to pass through on their honeymoon, so she'll find out soon enough.

No sense worrying her for something that can't be changed in the meantime."

"Smart girl. Feeling better?"

"Not only am I feeling better, I'm not nearly so hormonal. You're like my magic drug." I started to get up. He kept me on his lap.

"I'll fix you dinner," I said.

"I'm not particularly hungry. Why don't we go down to the Amber Rose and give Sam the good news?"

"Why don't we do that in the morning?" I asked. "In the meantime, why don't we retire early so you can refresh my memory on how I got into this condition in the first place?"

"I'll see if I can remember," he said, standing with me in his arms. "And then I'll spend the rest of my life reminding you."

"Have I mentioned lately that you're my hero, John Franklin Montgomery?"

"Not that I recall. It's that old faulty memory again. Let's take some time for you to show me what that means." He softly pushed the door closed behind us.

To read more about the lives of Callie and Jack, be sure to read Jordan and Brandan's story in Thunder Struck, Book 2 in the *Thunder on the Mountain* Series.

BEHIND THE STORY

Growing up on shorelines, I ached for the sound of crashing waves when I went away to college in Boulder, CO. Coming around a mountain pass one day, my heart sang at the sight of a wide expanse of water, and from that moment on, Nederland became my favorite haunt.

Months later, sitting in a snowstorm in my car, watching angry whitecaps form on Barker Reservoir in Nederland, I had my first experience with thundersnow, a strange phenomenon of thunder reverberating in the confined space of heavy snow clouds. When I decided to write my first book, I used a profession I knew (Realtor), and a place I loved (Nederland), and the *Thunder on the Mountain* series was born.

Looking at a book of Frank Lloyd Wright homes one day, I thought of his three names, thought of a name that had a nickname that was different than the actual name (John/Jack), and thought about what would happen if you knew of someone on a deep level but didn't really know them. John Franklin Montgomery was born.

Honest reviews are always helpful. If you would be willing to take a moment to review Thunder Snow (or any of Mimi Foster's other books), it would be greatly appreciated.

AUTHOR REQUEST

In this day and age of eBooks, eReaders, Amazon, Kindle, Barnes & Noble, Goodreads, and similar venues, Reader Reviews are the lifeblood of today's authors.

If you would be willing to take just a minute before you go and leave an honest review at the vendor from whom you purchased this book, and/or on Goodreads, it would be helpful and very much appreciated.

And if you loved this story, be sure to sign up at Mimi Foster Books to find out when the next book is scheduled for publication.

EXCERPT FROM THUNDER STRUCK

Book 2 in the Thunder on the Mountain Series

As Andrew took my face in his hands and kissed me on the fore-head, nose, and lips, there was no way I could have known that my whole world would be turned upside down by this time tomorrow.

"So I'll see you for lunch?" he asked.

"That works for me. I have a dress fitting and a few errands in the morning, but I can meet you at The James by noon."

"You sure you won't stay the night? I promise I'll make it worth your while."

"Three more weeks, then we have the rest of our lives. And I have to admit, I'm enjoying our new playfulness. How are you holding up?"

"Come home with me and I'll show you," he said, pulling me tight against him.

"You're incorrigible."

He took my face once more and gave me his special kiss. We had made the decision to not sleep together the last month before the wedding, and our relationship was benefiting from a fresh degree of flirtatiousness.

What a whirlwind it had been. With the planning and arrangements of our upcoming vows and honeymoon, and the sale of my New York co-op, I'd taken an extended leave of absence from the law firm.

An associate who was out of town for a month let me sublet her apartment, and somewhere in the mix I even inherited a Bed and Breakfast in a tiny town in Colorado. I'd done research on the mountain village where it was located, and hoped to talk Andrew into a side trip during our travels. It sounded romantic.

The past few years had been twelve-hour days with little down time, so this working vacation was a coveted time to unwind. I had turned my case files over to Andrew and could easily fill him in if he had questions. It sometimes surprised me that we'd been able to build a relationship, but our working proximity made it convenient, and he had been persistent.

"Good evening, Jordanna." I loved that my father called me by my given name. He had answered the phone in his distinctive, clipped voice. "Ready to come back to work?"

"Not a chance, but thanks for the offer," I said affectionately. "I'm calling to let you know I've cleared my schedule and turned everything over to Andrew. I brought him up-to-date on my case-load, so if you have questions, you can check with him."

"Are you sure he's up to the task?"

"You're not?" I was slightly surprised at his question.

"Oh, don't get me wrong. He seems competent enough, but he doesn't hold a candle to Jordanna Olivia. I trust your judgment, however, so if he's going to be my son-in-law, I'll commence showing him the inner sanctum of Whitman and Burke."

"I appreciate your vote of confidence. He's clever at handling my clients in a savvy and capable manner."

"That's never been a question, but I'll start giving him more responsibility. Don't be a stranger. Stop in when you're around. Maybe we can do lunch next week? Call Carol and set something up."

"Of course. Thank you, Father."

The early September air was brisk and added a degree of bounce to my step. I had a list of things I wanted to accomplish before I met Andrew for lunch. We were meeting a realtor afterwards to look at a Brooklyn Brownstone we were interested in purchasing.

Finishing two errands, I was lighthearted with my newfound freedom as I entered the third store. The boutique was elegantly subdued and had been highly recommended. I wanted lingerie for our wedding night, and the garden-level provided just the right amount of light and privacy for intimate apparel shopping.

Coming out of the fitting room, I saw Andrew through the tinted window leaving the building across the street. Surprised and pleased to see him, I started to call out when I remembered my scanty attire. Hurrying to the dressing room, I grabbed my phone and headed back to the window to text him and let him know where I was.

He turned just then toward the blonde who walked out behind him. Their lips almost touched, and I thought I was mistaken that it was Andrew, so I set down my phone.

He held her face in his hands and kissed her forehead, nose, and lips. The breath left my body. His arms embraced the fair-haired beauty who laid her head on his chest as he stroked her in the all-too-familiar way he had done to me so often. I tried to reactivate my brain to grasp what to do next.

Think, Jordan, think. Seconds passed before the adrenaline surged and I became somewhat coherent and focused. I grabbed a robe from a nearby hook and quietly opened the door. Magnifying my phone camera for a close up, I was able to capture several pictures of Andrew holding her face and kissing her before they slowly broke apart. I stepped back and let the door close, imagining it was closing on a huge part of my life.

Shocked as though hit by an electric current, I was still able to text to say something had come up and I wouldn't be able to meet, and asked him to cancel our appointment. Watching as he received the message, he immediately ran to catch up with the blonde. He put his arm around her as they walked away.

Was it possible I was mistaken? The photos told me the truth. I'd been kissed like that too many times to not understand that life as I knew it had been radically altered, and my world was going to be rocked to its foundation. It was all I could do to hold myself together.

The clerk was sweet when I told her something had come up and I'd have to leave without purchasing her diaphanous creations. Alternating between disbelief and anger, I was unsure where to go, what to do. Was there protocol for something like this? The more I wandered, the angrier I got.

I wasn't aware of the miles I walked, but by the time I found myself in front of the advertising agency of my best friend, I was ready to detonate. How do you share this information? When does the trembling stop?

"What is it? What happened?" Jeni said, coming around the desk, taking me by the shoulders.

Too angry to be coherent, I pulled my phone from my purse and showed her the pictures. I saw awareness dawn, then indignation washed over her. "I was going to make excuses, think maybe you were wrong, maybe it's his cousin, maybe it's not him, but it's Andrew, isn't it?" she asked with fire in her eyes.

Nodding, I wanted to fling something. It unnerved me that I never saw it coming. I now understood the term 'blindsided.' A thousand questions, and they all came back to, "Was this my fault?"

"Don't you *dare* go there, Jordanna Olivia Whitman! This is *his* fault! You will not share an ounce of guilt, do you hear me?"

"It's not guilt, it's self doubt and anger and disbelief and stupidity in not seeing. What if I had *married* him? And the questions keep coming. How long has it been going on? Who is she? What did he want from me? But I can't seem to get away from, *How could I have been so stupid?"*

"You had no way of knowing. I can be done for the day. Let's get out of here."

As we headed down the elevator, she asked, "What are you going to tell him? Surely you're calling off the wedding?"

"There's no way I can talk to him right now. I'm seeing red. And of *course* I'm calling off the wedding. I'm just not sure where to go now that I sold my co-op. How do you avoid the gigantic spotlight that'll find you when news like this breaks?"

"You can stay at my place. You know me, I'll put a favorable spin to it."

"I wouldn't think of putting you through something like that. God, Jeni, it's going to be awful."

"Jordan! Remember the letter you got last month about a Bed and Breakfast in some obscure little town? Where was that, Wyoming? Colorado? Did you ever respond?"

"People would think I was running away."

"Who gives a rip what anyone thinks? You've got lots of time off. You get to do what you want, especially right now."

"Having a drink sounds like a good option," I suggested hopefully.

"Sounds perfect. Come on."

We drank at several bars, but somewhere along the way I lost count of how many. I *was* aware, however, that with each successive stop, the funny side of today's surprise took hold. We were relaxed and silly by the time we got back to my temporary condo.

"I mean seriously, Jeni, what were the chances I'd be standing right there, right then? Kismet."

The familiar ding of Andrew's text came through. *Sorry you couldn't make it for lunch. I was so lonely without you. Want to meet for drinks?*

Can't make it. Out with Jeni. Will be in touch. Maybe you can find something else fun to do.

Nothing's fun without you.

I couldn't even respond. What a snake. How long had he been seeing her? It didn't look as though they'd just met.

"Wanna spend the night with me, Jeni? There's an extra room. My clothes fit you. In the morning we're either on the same page, or you'll talk me down from the cliff. Please?"

"We're diabolical plotters. Of course I will." We broke into laughter again.

"And you know what else?" I asked after a few minutes of silence. "I was excited about owning a Brownstone."

"Isn't *that* the truth? You might still want to, you just have to wait 'til the dust settles from *this* fallout before you think about taking a major step like that."

Lying on the couch a while later, she asked, "How do you feel? I'm ready to tear him limb from limb. What are *you* thinking?"

"Not a clue. The idea of going to Nederland has some appeal."

"Okay, but we don't decide anything 'til morning," Jeni said. "It's been a long day and your world derailed. We're not necessarily coherent, so let's see how you feel after a good night's sleep."

The morning dawned clear. Surprisingly, so did my brain. With Jeni's encouragement, I was warming to the idea of leaving town. "Not sure where the letter ended up in the confusion of my move, but I remember the name of the realtor that the lawyer mentioned I should contact in case I wanted to sell the place. I'll call her and get whatever details I need. In the meantime, we have to notify guests, figure out what to do with the gifts, the caterers, the travel arrangements, hotels . . . the plans."

I'd never considered myself vindictive, but I was ready to proceed. Jeni and I spent the day contacting caterers and venues and making the necessary arrangements to cancel a wedding that had been in the planning stages for months. Then we went to a print shop and waited while we had 'unvitations' printed, as Jeni was calling them. My marketing pal had done a great job designing them.

It was Saturday evening. I had a plane ticket to Denver for Monday noon. I made contact so I knew how to meet the realtor, Callie Weston, when I got there. I hadn't spoken with Andrew since the events of yesterday morning. What surprised me was I didn't feel sad about it. I was angry and embarrassed, but I didn't feel a loss yet. Time away would help me gain perspective. There was no part of me that felt a need to answer his calls. I returned his texts to tell him I was spending the weekend with Jeni attending to wedding matters and would contact him Monday, all of which was true. It's not like he was pining for me.

"I think it's poetic justice," Jeni said, "but I don't have as much at stake as you do. Sure you want to go through with this?"

"Telling my father will be the worst, but I'm sure he'll find a way to put the famous Wiley Riley twist on it. We both know how adept he is at that sort of thing."

"No question, he's the master. Okay, sweetheart, let's get these addressed."

Everything was in place by early Monday. Arrangements had been canceled and the unvites were ready for Jeni to drop in the mail. She was a trooper, staying with me the whole time, talking me through the ups and downs, helping me get the details done. Most important had been her encouragement that life was going to be deliciously different soon. I had one last stop to make before my flight.

Knowing he was at work, I used my key to let myself into

Andrew's apartment. My purpose was twofold: to make sure I had all my belongings from his place, and to leave him a copy of the unvite so he'd have a clue of what was about to hit him.

Jeni and I discussed the pros and cons of giving him warning, but it was all the more appealing to think he would know beforehand and there wouldn't be a thing he could do to stop it. I had momentary twinges of doubt about whether or not to go through with it until I saw two wine glasses in the sink, one with a lipstick imprint. I had made the right decision. Much harder would be the phone call to my father during the cab ride.

As Jordan was landing at Denver International Airport, Andrew was arriving home after a tiring day. They hadn't spoken in a while, but he recognized her handwriting on the distinctive envelope on the counter. He immediately looked around, hoping nothing was out of place, and made a mental note to remember to be more careful in the future.

It was strange that her key was on the counter. "Jordan?" he called out. "You here?" He let out a sigh of relief as he reassured himself everything appeared to be in order - until he picked up the letter and noticed it was propped against two wine glasses, one with the betrayal of red lipstick on its rim. Tearing open the envelope, he saw the bold, perfect lettering that proclaimed: *LOVE IS BLIND*. He fell into a chair as he opened the card to see an intimate picture of him kissing Mary Ann with large letters announcing: *FORTUNATELY, I'M NOT.*

If you've enjoyed reading any of these books, please consider leaving a review. And I love to hear from readers, so drop me a line at mimi@mimifoster.com or follow me on my website MimiFosterBooks.com.

CURRENT BOOKS

By Mimi Foster

THUNDER SNOW – Contemporary
Thunder on the Mountain Series Book 1 – stand alone
Jack and Callie
An admired but reclusive businessman wants nothing to do with emotional entanglements. When a self-sufficient redhead invades his sanctuary, he must set aside his past to protect her from a stalker bent on destruction.

THUNDER STRUCK – Contemporary
Thunder on the Mountain Series Book 2 – stand alone
Brandan and Jordan
*Betrayed New York lawyer escapes to an isolated town. As she and a local builder remodel a Victorian mansion, they find old journals that mirror the present as history begins repeating itself. (**MADELINE MANOR** is the "sweet" version.)*

THUNDER STORM – Contemporary
Thunder on the Mountain Series Book 3 – stand alone
Miles and Jeni

A blaze of fascination ignites each time the zany New York ad executive and a hunky Colorado contractor meet, but neither is willing to get involved in a long distance relationship.

JORDAN'S GIFT – Historical Novella
Thunder on the Mountain Series Book 4 – stand alone
Edward and Jordan
A hardened mine owner has little tolerance for people until he encounters a fiery newcomer who is running from the conventions of society and a broken engagement to his archrival. He will do anything to protect her from the smooth talking, black hearted, jilted fiancé.

WILLOW'S SECRET – Historical
Thunder on the Mountain Series Book 5 – stand alone
Charles and Willow
She's too busy for daydreams of handsome heroes, but a generous, well-respected railroad heir has no shame in fanning the fiery flames of attraction that spark every time he and the vibrant young woman are near each other.

STEALING RUNNER'S HEART - Contemporary
Leaving the Game Series Book 1 - stand alone
Runner and Charlotte Rose
When she was a child, he was her hero. When she grew up, he was her dream. When he brings home a fiancé, Charlotte is determined to carve out a new life for herself. But before the final curtain falls, is it worth one more chance to go after what she wants before her dreams are extinguished forever?

MAISY'S MIRROR – Contemporary
Non-series – stand alone
Wills and Maisy
A young widow living in seclusion buys an antique mirror and falls in love with a handsome reflection who shares an intriguing tale of love and

betrayal. Will she find the strength to convey his story to release him from his ethereal prison and from her life?

I love to hear from readers, so drop me a line at mimi@mimifoster.com or follow me on my website MimiFosterBooks.com.

ABOUT THE AUTHOR

Bestselling writer of romance novels in the early morning hours, award-winning Realtor during the day, Mimi is an incurable romantic who loves to create sexy but tender escapes about unforeseen encounters that forever alter lives for the better.

In addition to being married to her perfect human, Mimi is a blogger and photographer. She made five perfect female humans (her greatest achievement). They, in turn, have made five more small perfect humans.

She loves to hear from readers, so be sure to find her on her website (MimiFosterBooks.com), or interact with her on social media.

BB bookbub.com/authors/mimi-foster

f facebook.com/mimifosterbooks

○ instagram.com/ByMimiFoster

www.ingramcontent.com/pod-product-compliance
Lightning Source LLC
Chambersburg PA
CBHW060151130626
46556CB00006B/2595